The Warm Taste

A Vampire Coffee Shop Romance

Julia Leijon

Can a dark creature find a home in the light?

Robin appears to be a quiet, attractive young man, but the exterior hides his true vampire nature: ageless, unchanging, and bloodthirsty. His current obsession is Martin, the personable and generous owner of a coffee shop, The Warm Taste.

All Robin's careful plans to remain unnoticed are ruined, however, when Martin asks him out on a date.

Can Robin really have something so good and sweet as an ordinary relationship, after such a long existence of cold loneliness? And if things fall apart, and Robin goes back to his old ways, will Martin survive it?

Full of deliciously explicit sex scenes, this novel truly lives up to its name: dark, sweet, and just the thing to satisfy a craving.

Published by
NineStar Press
PO Box 91792
Albuquerque, New Mexico, 87199
www.ninestarpress.com

Print ISBN # 978-1-945952-04-3
Cover by Natasha Snow
Edited by Elizabeth Coldwell

Dedication

For Maria, Elsie, and Izzy

Acknowledgements

Deepest thanks to Karin Simon, for translating the German edition, Jacqueline Sweet, for the cover art on the German edition, Elizabeth Coldwell for editorial work on the NineStar Press edition, and Natasha Snow for cover art on the NineStar Press edition. All of you made this story much shinier than it could have been without you.

Chapter One

Robin

It was well past evening. The windows of the coffee shop spilled warm golden light out onto the cold sidewalk. Robin's breath didn't steam on his exhales, and the temperature of the air didn't bother him, but he wore a bulky coat and scarf for show.

He'd learned years ago that if he made sure that the people around him had no reason to notice him—if his dress was seasonal, his manner unremarkable—then he was forgotten almost before he was gone. It was possible to behave in a very inhuman fashion without drawing attention, provided he at least looked the part.

Most of the patrons inside the coffee shop at this hour were students from the local college, studying late. The campus was nearby, and it was still early enough in the semester for all the young scholars to look fairly bright-eyed and confident, not panicked and exhausted like they would when more weeks had passed.

The light inside was bright enough that Robin couldn't see even a faint reflection of his own face in the glass of the door. If it had been darker inside than out, there would have been a mirror image, despite what superstitions about vampires usually said. Robin knew well enough what he looked like.

His eyes were blue, with enough gray lurking in the color that they could pick up a tint of green if there was a particularly vivid shade nearby. His hair was blond and he wasn't tall, or broad-shouldered, which could have had the effect of making him look even younger than his unchanging eighteen years, if not for the confident grace he'd always had to his movements.

To those who only met him briefly, Robin probably appeared around the same age as those college students on the other side of the glass; just starting out toward the world of adult life before the cynicism set in.

If anybody knew him for a longer length of time, they would have begun to see flashes of hardness and darkness in his sweet, fine-boned face; flashes that made him look much, much older. But Robin made sure nobody ever knew him for long enough to notice things like that.

He pushed the door open, the wave of warmth and sound reaching out onto the cold street to envelop him and draw him into the small enclave of life inside.

Martin was behind the counter because Robin wouldn't have bothered visiting the coffee shop in the first place if it had been the man's single weekly night off. Robin had taken the time to learn Martin's schedule, in order to avoid unnecessary ventures out into the living world. There was no point in spending time among the students and their books and coffees unless Martin was there.

His knowledge of Martin extended beyond knowing the man's working days. Little facts and slivers of information had been collected by Robin, piece by piece, until he'd managed to build up a comprehensive picture of the coffee shop's attractive, personable owner.

Martin was thirty-five years old. He didn't have any brothers or sisters, and had lost his parents in his early twenties, coming into a considerable insurance payout when they died. That money remained largely untouched, however, with Martin only dipping into the funds once in all the time he'd had it. That had been when he'd bought the coffee shop. He'd named it The Warm Taste and had worked there ever since.

He had brown eyes and brown hair with the first glints of silver shot through it. He was tall and lean; his body kept in shape through energetic games of Frisbee and fetch with his dog on days off.

Robin liked Daniel's dog. She was a black-and-white fox terrier cross with a truly obnoxious personality, barking viciously at innocent bystanders as if they were dire threats but instantly cowering from the slightest hint of real danger. She had Martin wrapped around her metaphorical little finger; he would have done anything for that rotten little brat. It made Robin smile to watch.

The dog's name was Nora, and she liked Robin. Dogs always liked Robin. They noticed him much more often than people did.

Robin approached The Warm Taste's counter. He glanced up at the chalkboard hanging suspended from the ceiling and displaying the various beverage options. Reading through the choices was just habit, because he always ordered a cappuccino with one sugar. Observation of the coffee shop's patrons had taught him that this was the most commonly ordered drink, which therefore made it the least individual and the easiest to forget.

Robin didn't want to be remembered. He made a point of having as little impact on human lives as possible. On the occasions when he'd been weak-willed, and given Martin reason to have strong recollection of him, Robin had later, with utmost care, mesmerized the man. Made him forget.

If anybody had known Robin's habits well enough to comment on them, they would have called him fastidious. Nobody did, though. Robin was careful to make sure that was the case, as well. The more solitary he was, the less complicated his existence remained. So long as nobody knew him, nobody was affected by

3

him.

Robin's natural inclination to thrive on chaos was not a recipe for longevity, and so he'd forced himself to learn how to appreciate an existence that ran smoothly.

"Cap with one sugar, right?" Martin asked, interrupting Robin's moment of introspection.

Robin blinked in surprise. Martin shouldn't remember him at all; much less have his order memorized.

Martin was giving him an easy, friendly smile, waiting for confirmation of the order. "Y-yes," Robin stammered, thrown by the situation. He handed over his money and moved away from the counter hurriedly, seating himself at a table in the corner.

He'd never had that happen before.

His hands, usually steady and still, were shaking. It had been a very long time since anything had managed to unnerve him. Robin found he did not like the reminder of what that particular sensation felt like.

"Here's your coffee," the shop's waitress said as she placed Robin's order on the table in front of him. She gave him a friendly but impersonal smile, and left him alone again.

That was Sarah. Robin had never bothered to wipe clean any memories Sarah might have had of him. He'd been able to tell from the first time he'd visited the coffee shop that Sarah was someone who was very good at minding her own business, like he tried to be.

There was a cozy rhythm to The Warm Taste's operation. The *thunk-thunk-thunk* of spent coffee being knocked free, the hiss of heating milk, the scent of each fresh order. Some of the tables, those with groups seated around them, were sites of conversation, and each opening of the door let in the soft sounds of the night street outside with its cars and trams and pedestrians.

Sarah's young daughter arrived, looking over toward where

Robin sat and then leveling a stormy glare directly at him. Before he had a chance to puzzle over the meaning of the thunderous expression, Sarah went over and gave her child a hug of greeting.

"Mom, there's someone in my seat," the girl complained, shooting another scowl at Robin. He shrank lower in his chair, wondering if he should move somewhere else.

"You don't pay rent on it. It isn't yours," Sarah answered cheerfully, gesturing to one of the still-unoccupied tables. "Sit there instead."

"But that one is my one. I always sit there."

"Hey, Polly," Martin called from behind the counter. "I've got cinnamon buns and donuts on offer today. Which do you want?"

While the girl was distracted by making her selection from the food on offer, Robin quickly disposed of his order and exited the coffee shop. He didn't want to cause trouble. He didn't want to cause anything.

It would only be a few hours until closing time. It would be just as easy to spend it out here, in the shadows of the surrounding nine-to-five stores with their lightless interiors, as it would have been to remain inside. Easier, in fact, because out here there was nobody to notice him. Only fast-walking pedestrians who never looked his way at all.

Robin waited, unmoving, as the time ticked past.

Eventually, Martin emerged from the now-darkened coffee shop, swathed in his own scarf and coat, the last to go home as always.

Robin had tried, in the past, to have conversations with Martin at this juncture. Something always ruined it, sooner or later. Martin would notice that Robin's breath didn't steam as his own did, or Robin would find himself too caught up in Martin's friendly conversation and forget to be sufficiently careful with his own words. It was easier to do things the way he did now.

Robin stepped forward, blocking Martin's path. Before the man had the chance to do more than give a start of surprise, Robin had made eye contact with him, their gazes locked together with all the power of a meeting between predator and prey.

It was simple enough for Robin to bewitch humans in this fashion. There wasn't any real magic behind it; it was merely the power of an extremely persuasive vocal cadence and unwavering eye contact combining to create a powerful hypnotic suggestion. It was an evolutionary advantage bestowed on those with the unfortunate luck to have been turned into vampires.

"Don't notice me. I'm not here," Robin instructed Martin in quiet, lilting tones. Martin gave a small nod, his posture the slightly slack carriage of someone not completely aware or awake. "Now go home."

Martin shook himself, roused from the trance, and glanced around. He had a perplexed expression on his face. His eyes didn't pause for even a moment as they looked past Robin and moved on. Robin was as good as invisible, completely unregistered by Martin now.

Martin lived in the same neighborhood as his coffee shop, only fifteen minutes away on foot. He owned a car, but Robin had never known him to drive it. It was clear he liked the quiet interlude of time spent walking to and from his business each day.

Despite Martin being right there next to him, albeit oblivious to his presence, Robin felt oddly lonely as they moved through the darkened, sparsely populated streets toward Martin's home. It was idiotic to feel this way, of course. Robin had more sentimentality in him than was good for him. He really must make the effort to discard such absurd thoughts.

Loneliness. What an absurd notion for a vampire. Loneliness was for wolves or lions, denied a pack or pride. Vampires were solitary hunters. Their very nature was to be alone.

Nora the dog barked noisily as Martin unlocked his front door. Robin's mouth curved up into a small, brief smile. He was irrationally fond of the irritating little animal, and enjoyed seeing how she and Martin doted on one another.

After greeting Nora, Martin took off his scarf and coat and hung them on a hat stand positioned near the front door. Robin left his own on. Temperature made no difference to him.

The sight of Martin's now-exposed neck made Robin's mouth water.

"Sit on the sofa," he ordered the man, his voice a little ragged and raw to his own ears. Martin did so, walking through to the living room area and resting against the cushions with a tired sigh. Robin followed, kneeling on the sofa beside where Martin sat.

Nora trotted in after them, taking up her habitual position on an armchair in the corner of the room, and began methodically shredding a small plush toy in the shape of a mallard duck. Robin couldn't help but laugh quietly at the sight. He wasn't sure which interpretation was funnier: either Nora considered him unthreatening, despite his blatantly predatory intentions toward her human, or her natural instincts as a coward made her determined to ignore the proceedings completely.

Forgetting about Nora for the time being, Robin turned his attention back to Martin. He tilted the man's head away from him, baring the smooth, warm skin of his throat.

Usually Robin hardly noticed his own fangs. They were barely longer than the teeth surrounding them, only an eighth of an inch or so of extra sharpness at their points. Now, however, they seemed to crowd his mouth, making it difficult for him to think of anything but biting down into that skin.

Instead of the deep bite that Robin's baser nature urged him to inflict, the strike he made was little more than a small, shallow nip, piercing the skin carefully and delicately. This way, he could drink for longer without bringing any kind of real harm to Martin.

Robin's face was cold from the night air, his body having picked up the ambient temperature of his surroundings on the walk to Martin's home. Robin hadn't been a source of heat in decades, ever since his death. He absorbed, never generated.

The touch of his lips to Martin's skin made a minute shiver run through the man, the skin of his arms pebbling into gooseflesh.

The reaction was an automatic response to the cold. If Robin was some other kind of predator, it might have been an instinctive reaction to a threat, but—in yet another case of fact running counter to superstition—vampires who intended to survive for any length of time hardly ever seriously harmed their quarries, let alone killed them.

They left no carnage, conjured no warmth. They were as invisible as thoughts.

Martin's blood was honey sweet over a whisper of iron, warm and slow and so good that Robin's eyes rolled back at the first taste of it on his tongue.

It took a considerable amount of self-control for him to resist the urge to suck at the little wound, but Robin was nothing if not well-versed in acts of considerable self-control. The cut itself, he'd be able to heal without trouble, but it would be unwise to leave any other kind of mark behind after he was finished.

Fuck, Martin tasted so good. Despite owning a coffee shop, he only drank a few cups of it each morning, typically switching to peppermint tea and water at midday. Robin, despite his extensive experience with people's blood, had no idea if any of that played any role in the taste of him. Perhaps Martin's chemistry was just perfectly, exactly aligned with Robin's own.

It was that taste that kept him coming back. It was incredibly dangerous to return to the same source of blood over and over like this, but he couldn't stop. He couldn't imagine contenting himself with another source, not while he knew Martin existed. Not while there was his exquisite blood somewhere in the world, there for the taking.

Robin repositioned himself, straddling Martin's lap in order to press himself closer. In his new posture he could inhale Martin's scent more deeply, drag his tongue against the welling cut on Martin's skin; lose himself in the experience.

He was so lost in it, in fact, that when Martin's hands moved up to fumble with the scarf still wrapped around Robin's own throat, it was a few moments before Robin realized what was happening.

Martin's fingertips sought the skin of Robin's neck and shoulder, stroking at it, urging him closer. The touch was like electricity on Robin's skin, thrilling and terrifying. Martin's fingers were combing through his hair, resting against the back of his skull, as Martin sighed contentedly.

It was good enough to drive Robin crazy. But, like any goodness that came into his life, it was a goodness he had stolen. Guilt and shame drained the pleasure from the moment, and Robin broke away from Martin's throat and sat back, forcing himself to stand up.

He pressed the pad of his thumb to the point of one of his fangs, breaking the skin and making a bead of his own dark blood well up. He pressed this against the little tear he'd made on Martin's neck. The skin began to heal together almost immediately, without leaving any sign that there had been a cut at all.

"Stay there," Robin ordered in a quiet voice, making his way into Martin's kitchen. He was thrumming with energy, his mouth still full of the taste of Martin's blood. This was always the worst moment; this was when the full weight of what a monster Robin was would weigh down on him.

The rest of the time, Robin had no strong feeling about his existence. He tried to avoid having strong feelings about anything, if he could at all help it, and this applied twofold to the sordid choices and actions he let himself make on a regular basis.

But in these moments, when the blood was warm and new inside him, and it was his responsibility to see to the well-being of someone at his mercy, it was difficult to remain remote. Reality crashed into him, and he felt as if he might suffocate under the weight of it—or would, if he had a genuine need to breathe.

From out of the refrigerator, he retrieved a carton of orange juice, a packet of sliced ham, and a tub of easy-spread butter. There was a loaf of whole wheat bread on the countertop, which Robin inspected to make sure it was still suitable to use—Martin's busy schedule meant that sometimes loaves didn't get eaten in time to prevent penicillin colonies from attempting to spawn.

The bread was mold-free, though, so Robin made Martin two ham sandwiches and poured him a glass of orange juice. Provided he gave Martin a strong suggestion to have eggs and spinach for breakfast the following morning, the combined iron content of the two meals would help Martin's body replace what Robin had taken.

He took the food to Martin and ordered him to eat, waiting as the command was carried out. Even that gave Robin new waves of guilt, because watching Martin chew and swallow each bite mechanically, not truly tasting what he ate, was like stealing from him a second time.

Martin had a grand, all-encompassing enthusiasm for life. To take even the small, simple pleasures of a sandwich from him proved what an irredeemably evil creature Robin was.

When Martin had finished eating, Robin washed the plate and glass and left them in the kitchen, returning to his original spot on the sofa beside Martin.

"Look at me," he said. His eyes seized Martin's, transfixing Martin's gaze in the power of his own. Then Robin began to speak, repeating himself over and over, varying the words but always with the same message: *forget me. I was never here. You had a quiet evening, and now you're tired. You have no memory of me. You do not know that I exist.*

When Robin's voice began to go hoarse from speaking, he went quiet. Martin's eyes closed, and after a heartbeat's length of time he gave a wide and weary yawn.

Blinking, he rubbed at his face with his palms and got to his feet, shuffling toward the hallway that contained the bedroom and bathroom.

Nora jumped gracelessly from her position on her chair, trotting after Martin and leaving Robin alone in the room to do the last small tasks of cleaning up.

He straightened the sofa cushions, turned out the lights, and made sure the door locked behind him as he let himself out. There was no trace left behind that he'd ever been there at all.

It was even colder now, the last warmth of the day long faded. Robin paid no attention to the chill as he walked back to his own apartment, which was small and dark and empty.

☆☆☆

The following night, Robin didn't go to the coffee shop. He simply stayed in bed. He wasn't hungry anymore, so there was no reason to go anywhere. The hours felt excruciatingly long and exhaustingly short all at once. Robin simply waited for them to end and then slept again.

When the next evening began, Robin dragged himself from the bed, showered, and dressed. He had to make sure that Martin's memories had been properly fixed this time. He couldn't risk any future familiarity on visits to The Warm Taste.

If it hadn't worked for a second time, he knew that the only safe course of action would be to break contact entirely. The thought alone was enough to make him pause and close his eyes, overwhelmed with sudden panic.

There was no reason for his worry, though. When he entered the coffee shop and walked to the counter, Martin smiled at him with no hint of recognition in the expression.

"Welcome to The Warm Taste. What can I get for you?"

To his surprise, the question left Robin feeling strangely bereft.

Chapter Two

Martin

Friday night was always one of the busiest of the week, especially later in the evening. Couples out on dates stopped in for a drink together after the movies or plays they'd gone to were finished. And students, as always, chose proximity to coffee over the comparative quiet of the dorms or libraries.

This particular Friday night had been a good one. There hadn't been any major crises, and business was going great. Nevertheless, Martin knew that it would be nice to get home and fall into bed, resting his weary feet after a day of work. Doing busy shifts had been a damn sight easier when he was twenty-five years old than it was now he'd hit thirty-five.

Martin glanced at the clock. Fifteen minutes left until closing.

"Last call on orders, everyone," he announced to the room. "You've got a quarter of an hour left before we throw you all out, so if you want anything else, you'd better get it now."

A young man seated at one of the tables against the far wall of the shop rose from his seat and started walking toward the door. He paused to throw away his disposable cup, and as it fell into the trash bin Martin heard the telltale *thunk* that told him it was still full of coffee.

It was a tiny thing, not even that much of a rarity—people threw away far more coffee every day than Martin wanted even to think about. But for some reason he couldn't tear his eyes away from the young man. There was just something that held his attention captive, though it wasn't anything Martin knew how to describe. All he knew was that it was real, and it was there.

Then customers hoping for one last caffeine hit began approaching the counter, and by the time Martin could look back over to where the young man had been, he'd left, off into the dark beyond the coffee shop's door.

On the nights that followed, Martin started paying attention to the young man, motivated by more than the simple passing physical attraction he felt. It was as if there was a magnetic force, pulling Martin in, impossible to fight against and completely inevitable. It was a disconcerting feeling, and one unlike anything he could remember ever experiencing before.

Each night, the same pattern repeated: the young man would come in, buy a drink—and never the same order twice, Martin noticed. It was almost as if he was going out of his way to be unknowable, with even his coffee preferences kept absolutely private—then he would sit at one of the peripheral tables for most of the evening.

Just sitting, watching people. He'd never take even the smallest sip of the drink in his hands, merely holding the cup between his palms long past the point where the heat must have drained away from the liquid inside. At first, Martin had worried that the young man would burn himself, holding the hot drink like that, but he never seemed to be bothered, so it must be all right.

Martin wondered if the guy was lonely.

The following week flew by, and it was Friday again almost before he knew it. Martin's life was generally a pleasant one, and time passed easily in circumstances like that.

The rain that had been pelting down earlier in the day cleared up in the evening, leaving behind a sharp, fresh chill in the air. The interior of the shop was warm and noisy, as always, though on this particular occasion the general din included a new strain of disagreement between Sarah and Polly, the latter of whom was fast becoming skilled at the art of adolescent fussing.

"Moooooooooooom, it's Friday night. It doesn't matter if I'm up until dawn," Polly complained, her face conveying that her current ill-treatment at the hands of her mother was the greatest injustice any human had ever suffered throughout all of history. "Please can I have an iced coffee? Please."

"You can have iced chocolate. If you stop whining."

Polly pouted. "Fine."

Martin waved his hand, gesturing for her to return to her table. "I'll bring it over."

The girl dragged her feet as she walked back to her chair. Sarah gave a quiet, amused snort of laughter.

"I've never seen anyone look so oppressed over being given a free iced chocolate before."

Martin glanced at Polly's table. She'd forgotten she was meant to be sulking and was playing a game on her phone instead.

"I'm not sure if she even likes the taste of coffee," Sarah went on. "I think she only asks for it because she has an idea in her head that it makes her look sophisticated and grown-up."

Polly was very small for her age, a lifetime of bad health leaving her with a delicate, petite frame and a sweet, young face that made her look closer to eight years old than to her actual age of twelve. Martin knew it was a sore point for the kid, so as far as he could see, anything that made her feel like her own age—or like the age that girls her age liked to pretend they were—was all right. He grinned.

"People have developed coffee habits for worse reasons," he told Sarah. That made her grin, too.

"Tell me about it. I never would have got my GED without my mom's crappy little coffee maker. It helped me through more than one all-nighter."

Sarah had been working at The Warm Taste since her late teens, almost as long as the shop had been open. Technically she was Martin's shift supervisor, despite him being the owner—she'd made it to General Manager in a very short span of time after arriving, thanks to a brain that was naturally organized to a level Martin ruefully knew he'd never achieve himself.

Right from when he'd first opened the coffee shop, Martin had always tried to employ kids around college age. Occasionally, for some of the part-time positions, he'd take on actual students, if they seemed like they really needed the money. Mostly, though, he chose townies like Sarah. He hoped it did both groups good to mix.

Sarah had blonde hair and hazel eyes. Polly's hair was a few shades darker, and of a finer texture—like everything about Polly, there was a thin, breakable quality to the long braid down her back. The two of them were close, though Martin had noticed a glimmer of teenage sassiness creeping into Polly's interactions with her mother over the past few months. He had a feeling they were in for a fairly tumultuous adventure together over the next decade or so.

Martin glanced at Polly again. She was still absorbed in her game. Then he shifted his attention, sneaking a surreptitious look at the young man with the mysterious drinking habits.

The young man was watching him, gazing too intently to break away immediately when Martin's eyes met his own. Martin offered what he hoped was a warm smile, and the young man looked down at the table with equal intensity as if he was shy about being caught out. No blush colored his cheeks, though; they remained as porcelain pale as ever. So maybe it was all right.

Hoping this wouldn't frighten him away for good, Martin left the counter and went over to where he sat.

"You don't need to keep buying orders you don't want, you

know," Martin said. "I'm not going to throw you out, if you just want to be around people. It's not like we're ever packed full at night. You're a pretty low key customer; I don't mind if you stay without buying anything."

The look on the young man's face was almost like panic. Did he hate his existence being acknowledged that much? If that was the case, Martin's heart went out to him. Nobody should ever prefer being invisible.

"What's your name?" he asked, keeping his voice as friendly as he could, and hoping he wasn't pushing too hard. Martin wanted the guy to keep visiting the coffee shop, not run away in terror at being noticed and never dare to return.

"Robin. You're Martin." It was difficult to read the emotions underlying his soft, well-spoken words, but Martin thought he sounded sad. Wistful.

"There, now we know each other." Martin smiled. "And since we know each other, you can stay here without buying things."

Not wanting to overwhelm the guy with too much interaction all at once, Martin left him alone after that.

The rest of the evening was unremarkable, and before Martin knew it his watch was buzzing noisily from the alarm he'd set on it earlier.

"I'm going to head off now. You gonna be okay for the rest?" Martin asked Sarah, ninety minutes before the coffee shop's usual closing time. She nodded, shooing him toward the door.

"I won't run you out of business in an hour and a half. Go lavish affection on that weird little rat you call a dog."

"Hey!" Polly, overhearing them, looked incensed. "Nora's a great dog! You take that back."

"I don't know how you brainwashed my kid, Mart, but clearly you've got powers."

"I'm a black magic hypnotist. I mesmerized her with my evil

spells," Martin agreed amicably. "See you later, Pol. You should come round sometime soon and play with Nora. She loves it when you visit."

As Martin walked past Robin's table, Robin stood, picking up a disposable cup that Martin was willing to bet was as full as it had been when it was first put on the table in front of him. Martin waved a hand, gesturing for him to stop.

"No, no, sit. You don't have to leave. I've told Sarah you're able to stay as long as you want. I'm going early because it was raining really hard before I came in to do my shift, and I have a dog that I couldn't take for a walk because of it. The stupid little monster has probably shredded everything chewable in the house while I've been out, with all that energy she didn't get a chance to burn off." Martin grinned. "It'll be hell to pay if I don't get to walk her tonight, trust me. See you around, Robin."

☆☆☆

Nora had, indeed, caused extensive mayhem in his absence. He took her on a long walk, knowing that she'd be happier to go even longer and it was only the cold that stopped them. Taking her out at night was actually less stressful than their usual walking time, because there weren't any perfectly blameless passersby for her to bark at threateningly.

"You are basically the worst dog in the world," Martin informed her. She gave him a wide doggy smile, tongue lolling.

☆☆☆

The next day was one of those comedy-of-errors days—Martin knocked over a glass of orange juice at breakfast; the power went off at The Warm Taste just before opening hours started and didn't come back on for forty-five minutes; he managed to slice a shallow cut into the ball of his thumb with a box-cutter while unpacking supplies in the storeroom; the only Band-Aids he could find were the ordinary long kind, which didn't sit securely on the palm of his hand; Sarah burned her arm on the milk thermometer, and a customer nearly had an allergic reaction because she hadn't expected the banana muffins to have walnuts and hadn't asked if they were safe.

It was the kind of day that was basically a write-off, and Martin was just waiting for it to be over. Everyone was frazzled and cranky, their routines thrown too out of whack by the barrage of small accidents for them to settle into their regular patterns of work.

When the time ticked closer to the hour when Robin usually appeared, Martin found himself glancing in the direction of the door more and more frequently. He felt silly for doing so, but couldn't help it all the same. After all the tiny mishaps, it would be nice for something good to happen.

Sure enough, Martin hadn't even been half waiting for twenty minutes before the door swung inward and Robin's ghost-pale coloring appeared. He glanced at the counter and then approached it, gaze fixed on Martin.

Robin's already unsettling eyes seemed almost lit from within, and they stared into Martin's as if they intended to capture his soul through sheer force of will.

"You and I should g—" he began to say to Martin in a low voice, the words chopped off into sudden silence by an almighty crash from the back room and a string of surprised, cranky curses from Sarah. For just a moment, the look on Robin's face seemed to turn thunderously, violently dark, but the expression was gone as instantly as it had appeared, so quickly Martin couldn't quite be sure it had been there at all.

Martin looked away from those penetrating, unnatural eyes. "One second," he told Robin, hurrying over to the door of the storeroom.

Sarah was surrounded by individually wrapped plastic cutlery sets, which had spilled down onto her head from a now mostly empty box on a shelf she'd been reaching up to.

"I'm fine," she assured Martin. "Getting unexpectedly rained on by knives and forks, but fine."

"This whole day never happened," he answered. "Sound good?"

"Agreed." Sarah nodded, and then sighed. "Gimme a second to pick these up and I'll be back out."

Martin gave a nod of his own in reply, returning to the counter where Robin was still standing.

"Do you want to go out some time?" Martin asked Robin before Robin had a chance to say a word.

Robin blinked at him. "What?"

"You. Me. A date? Maybe a movie?"

Robin blinked again, the confusion even more obvious on his face this time. "But I hadn't finished asking you yet. Why would you ask me?"

Martin felt as confused as Robin looked. "Because I thought we might have a good time together?"

"Oh." Robin's perplexed frown was endearing and sad at the same time. Did he really think it was so weird that Martin might be interested in him? And, if so, why would it have apparently made so much difference if Robin had been the one to ask him?

"Um. Yes. We should." Robin gave an awkward little nod. "That would be good."

"How about tomorrow night? We can meet at the cinema a couple of streets over from here. You know where that is?"

Robin nodded again, and then looked quizzical. "Don't you have to be here tomorrow night?"

Martin shrugged. "I often leave a bit early on the night before my day off. Makes it feel longer, y'know? How about we say seven, in the foyer?"

Without warning Robin gave a broad, bright grin. It completely transformed him, giving him a sweet-faced, youthful energy. Martin couldn't help but grin back.

"Yeah, okay," Robin said. "I'll see you there."

It was Martin's experience that going out, these days, typically meant the prospective couple would hang out with a larger group made up of the friends of one of the pair. That kind of setup didn't bother Martin the way he knew it did some guys his age. It took the pressure off; made things more casual.

Still, despite the group hangout being the usual dynamic for kids Robin's age, Martin wasn't all that surprised when he saw Robin waiting alone in the foyer of the movie theater. He'd never seen Robin sitting with anyone else at The Warm Taste, and had suspected for a while that the guy probably had a fairly solitary, maybe lonely, kind of life.

The movie was pretty forgettable; an action thriller about espionage that was more explosions than plot. Perfectly acceptable as a way to switch off critical thinking for a couple of hours, but not the kind of thing Martin would go out of his way to see under ordinary circumstances.

There hadn't been anything else all that appropriate playing at the complex, though, not unless the pair of them wanted to spend their first date watching a gross-out comedy or a cutesy tween flick that Martin was pretty sure even Polly would consider immature dreck.

Throughout the whole thing, Robin seemed on edge and jittery. His usual slightly flat affect had gone jagged, as if he was deeply apprehensive about something and anxious to get it over with.

"We could go out for a drink," he suggested, in much the same tone that Martin imagined other people might use to say, "I guess it's time to go be tortured now." Robin looked visibly hesitant at the idea of facing another crowded venue.

"We could have a drink at my place, if you like," offered Martin. Robin's relief at the invitation was almost comically obvious. Martin gave a sympathetic smile. "Not an extrovert, huh?"

"Yeah," Robin agreed. "Something like that."

☆☆☆

Nora galloped over to meet them as they came through the front door of Martin's home, jumping up to rest her paws as high as they would go on Martin's legs and then bounding over to do the same to Robin with a loud bark.

"That means she likes you, I think. It's hard to tell with her. She's pretty useless," Martin confessed. Robin laughed.

"Dogs usually like me. I guess I'm lucky that way."

"I had to look after one of my barista's dogs for a few months once," explained Martin, as Robin crouched down to rub her stomach when she offered it up for him. "Nora was the biggest brat in the world about it—she couldn't stand having to share my affection. If I was paying the slightest bit of attention to the other dog, she'd make a huge fuss and do her best to wedge herself in between my hand and the fur I was petting. And she'd deliberately drop toys right next to the other dog, so she had an excuse to pick a fight. That was one of her favorite tricks. Nora is pretty much the definition of 'does not play well with others.'"

"I guess it's a good thing she's an only child, then," Robin noted. Playing with Nora seemed to have at least temporarily cured him of a lot of the tension Martin had sensed in him earlier, but there was still a definite air of nervousness around him.

"We can just call it a night now, if you want," Martin told him, perturbed at the thought of Robin feeling pressured into doing anything he wasn't comfortable with.

"No! I mean..." Robin looked a little abashed at how adamant his reply was. He stood up, which made Nora snap her jaws pitifully, trying to recapture the love that had been showered on her seconds before.

"I mean," Robin tried again, stepping closer to Martin. "I want to stay for a while. Very much."

He pulled Martin into a hungry kiss, his smaller stature forcing Martin to bend down slightly in order for their mouths to meet. Making a soft, needy sound, Robin opened his mouth and licked at Martin's lips. Martin let him in, sucking on his tongue when it entered Martin's mouth.

Nora barked, loudly informing them of her annoyance over not being the center of their attention. The interruption made Martin give a snort of laughter. He broke off the kiss and tilted his head in the direction of the bedroom.

"C'mon, let's go get a little more privacy."

Martin liked his bedroom. He wasn't someone prone to lie-ins, or to spending much time in bed generally except for when he was asleep, so the contents of the room were fairly simple—double bed, built-in wardrobe, window. The simplicity gave the space a calming air, everything painted in soft autumnal shades. The bedspread was a deep mustard color, muted and inviting.

They were barely inside, the door shut behind them for privacy, before Robin sank to his knees, staring up at Martin with a gaze that burned.

There was always something arresting, heart-stopping, about the way Robin looked at him, and in that moment it was the look of someone yearning to the point of desperation.

"Let me?" he asked Martin. His voice was rough, as stripped bare as his expression.

Martin ended up sitting on the edge of the bed, with Robin kneeling between his now-bare legs. The room's overhead light was on but Robin's pupils were blown huge and black despite the brightness. Being wanted so much made Martin's breath uneven.

Robin's mouth against his cock was deliciously wet and curiously without heat. He didn't seem to believe in any kind of slow build, or teasing. Like everything else about him, Robin's sexual technique had a utilitarian efficiency about it. If not for the fact that he was also incredibly good at it, the whole thing might not have been particularly arousing.

He was so very, very good at it, however, that Martin's body felt as if it was being slammed into by unrelenting waves of lust. Robin was making small, greedy sounds; hums of pleasure as he sucked at Martin's cock. The vibration of where his hollowed cheeks and eager tongue were lying flush against Martin's sensitive skin was enough to make his hips buck up, or would have done if Robin wasn't holding him pinned with one hand.

Robin was surprisingly strong, Martin noted with one tiny corner of his thoughts, for someone who looked rather undernourished and weak.

Martin smoothed a hand over Robin's bobbing head, letting his fingers comb through fine-textured fair hair. It was almost doll-like, cool and shiny, more perfectly groomed than any other person Martin had ever met managed to keep their hair. Even movie stars didn't manage quite this level of unreal perfection.

Robin held Martin's hips down with both hands, preemptively pinning him in place on the edge of the mattress before an especially talented maneuver involving Robin's throat and lips. Martin cried out, the yell ripped straight from his lungs without his brain even knowing that it was going to happen.

"Robin," he managed to say, the word strangled and broken by the time it came out. "Oh, fuck, Robin, ah, ah, yes, like that, shit..."

Not his suavest pillow talk by a long shot, but Martin couldn't even attempt anything approaching coherency. He wasn't sure he'd even still remember what language was by the time they were done; all his higher brain functions were being enthusiastically sucked out of him.

Robin's eye contact never wavered, his dilated eyes staring up at Martin's without the slightest flicker, save for when one or the other of them had to close their eyes against the onslaught of pleasure for a moment.

Those eyes made Martin feel like every choice he'd made to bring him here had been a risky one. Usually, when he thought about getting caught up in something strange or otherworldly, his daydreaming involved being given a weird secret journal or notebook, and that would be the indicator he'd left normal life behind him. Or coded messages being whispered to him by mysterious, glamorous people he'd never met before. Something tangibly out of the ordinary; something signaling clearly that Martin had strayed from ordinary paths.

But Robin didn't need anything like that to make Martin feel that way. All he needed was his eyes. They were beautiful like a fire gone out of control was beautiful, like the pyramids of Egypt were beautiful, like the catacombs of Paris were beautiful. Awe-inspiring, terrifying; breathtaking in the most literal sense.

Robin's eyes made Martin feel like a creature, small and furred, that had the misfortune to cross paths with a tiger and now watched, frozen in its gaze, as it prepared to pounce.

Robin made Martin understand why the French called climaxing "the little death". The way Robin stared up at him with those dark-blown eyes had nothing to do with living, and everything to do with what came after.

Martin had never been so turned on in his life.

His whole existence, from running the coffee shop to looking after his dog, was all about nurturing and protecting. Martin's belly tightened, heat pooling heavily there and telling him that he was approaching the brink of orgasm. He stared down at Robin, watching those fathomless eyes. It was as if he'd met the counterpoint to himself, the being who existed by taking where he thrived on giving; the cold outside that defined the warm inside.

"Pull...pull away," Martin managed breathlessly. "I'm going to come."

Robin's lashes dropped low as he held Martin's hips down and took Martin's cock into his mouth down to the root. His throat convulsed rhythmically around him as Robin moaned, urging him on.

One of Martin's hands fisted the sheets of the bed where he sat, scrabbling at the fabric as if it could tether him to reality; hold him there despite the lust and need and want overwhelming him. With his other hand he found Robin's hair again, combing through its fine strands.

Robin moaned again, the sound making his throat vibrate around Martin's cock. Martin's fingers tightened reflexively in Robin's hair, pulling at those smooth locks without meaning to. The sharp pain, or maybe simply the surprise of the movement, made Robin moan even harder, his throat squeezing greedily.

That was enough to undo Martin completely. His hips tried to buck up as he came, but Robin held his hips in place. Robin's fine-boned cheeks were hollowed thin as he sucked and swallowed throughout Martin's climax, never breaking that searing eye contact.

When Martin was done, his cock gone too limp and sensitive for further touching, Robin rocked back on his heels. His lips were shiny and swollen. He looked wrecked. It was beautiful.

"Pull my hair again. Harder," Robin gasped out, wrapping one hand around Martin's wrist to hold it in place against his head.

Martin complied, tugging Robin's hair hard enough that it must have stung. Robin's body jerked, his eyes sliding closed in pleasure. The Band-Aid on the palm of Martin's hand tore free, the slice across the ball of his thumb splitting wide open. Hissing at the pain, he pulled his hand back, wincing as he saw the slippery smear of blood that had already managed to well out of the wound.

Robin's eyes snapped open.

"Shit, shit, I'm sorry," Martin said, trying to staunch the flow with his other hand and making even more of a mess. "Fuck. I'm sorry. You've got no idea if I've got anything you could catch through it. I mean, I don't, I get checked, but you've got no way of knowing that. Shit."

If it hadn't been such terrible, moment-destroying timing, Martin might have laughed at how spectacularly he'd managed to fuck up this date. He hadn't even thought about how they should have used a condom. He was just a disaster. It wouldn't have shocked him at all if Robin had hightailed it out of there.

Robin's hand shot out and grasped Martin's wrist a second time, holding it absolutely still. He was staring at the freely bleeding cut, his already blazing eyes looking even more weird and strange and bright in his face. His sex-plumped lips parted, and he leaned forward, running his tongue along the cut.

It should have stung and yet it didn't at all, even when Robin took Martin's thumb into his mouth and began sucking with as much enthusiasm and force as he had used on Martin's cock, at first with the flat of his tongue pressed against the welling blood at the base of the digit and then with his tongue tip probing at it, trying to press the cut wider so it would bleed more freely. A tiny growl rose from Robin's throat.

It felt so strange, completely alien and yet so familiar that a wave of déjà vu washed over Martin. He felt...pliant, his thoughts hazy and swimming, the pleasure very different to that of sex but completely unlike anything else that Martin might think of to compare it to.

It was such a pleasurable sensation that Martin gave a deep sigh, his free hand reaching out to touch Robin's face. It was hard to hold onto the confusion he felt over the whole situation; it slid away as slick and easy as the blood flowed. This felt right.

Robin readjusted his position, opening and then closing his mouth around the wound. In that moment Martin saw small fangs there, white and sharp as those of any vampire from a horror movie. Martin blinked in shock and surprise but felt no fear at the revelation. It was as if his world shifted, ever so slightly, and then fell back into place again with everything a perfect fit in its new position. Of course Robin was a vampire. That made sense.

Time passed, though Martin couldn't have said how much, before Robin sat back. For a moment, an expression of intense sadness clouded his features. It was the look of somebody forced to face up to a grim reality that gave them great distress.

Then, as fast as it had appeared, the expression vanished. Any strong emotion that had been visible on Robin's face fell away, leaving him unreadable and remote.

"Forget any of this. Forget me completely," he told Martin. His words were soft and liquid, the way some European accents could sound sometimes when their users spoke. "You won't remember this evening, or meeting me at The Warm Taste. Forget all of it."

There was a dreamy pull to the quiet litany, lulling Martin into wanting to agree to what Robin was telling him, and making him want to listen and surrender and obey.

He struggled to clear his mind, shaking his head back and forth as if to clear the comfortable fog that clouded his thoughts. Maybe it was the fact that the wound on his hand was finally beginning to sting, whatever numbing drug Robin had in his saliva wearing off. Or maybe it was just the amount of conscious attention he was paying to Robin; too much to be caught unawares.

Whatever the reason, Martin found that he could fight against the suggestions Robin's lyrical words were trying to plant into his subconsciousness.

"Mind control? Really?" He was almost too boggled to be serious about it. "Are you going to wear a black-and-red cape next? I'm not sure how it works in vampire dating, but humans are pretty big on informed consent when it comes to the kind of things we've been doing in here tonight, and mind control is basically the opposite of that. Do you really want to be that guy?"

Martin wasn't angry, which he felt a little surprised about. Probably, it would have been normal to be very, very angry. But all he felt was the need to make his refusal to tolerate it very clear.

"Listen carefully, because I am one hundred percent serious about this," he said to Robin. "You cannot ever try to do that to me again. For any reason. I need your absolute word on that. I don't like being manipulated. Do you understand?"

Robin, eyes wide, gave a silent nod. Then he swallowed and cleared his throat. "I understand."

Martin nodded as well, acknowledging the promise. The atmosphere in the room remained incredibly awkward for another few moments until Robin spoke again.

"I...you...you aren't angry. You aren't even scared." Robin's expression was confused to the point of distress. "Why aren't you scared of me? You should be scared of me."

Martin considered how to frame his answer before replying. The look on Robin's face was pulling at his heartstrings—that someone, anyone, could have such an absolute expectation of being responded to with horror and fear made Martin feel a deep sadness.

Instead of answering with words, Martin moved and shifted until Robin could see the ugly mess of scars on his back.

"From a belt, a cane, and a wire brush. There might have been other things, but those are the ones I remember," Martin told Robin. "Why should I be more afraid of you than anyone else? A person doesn't have to be a vampire to be capable of cruelty and violence. Those scars were made by my parents. They made me leave home in the end. They hated gay people more than they loved their only child. They sent me to conversion therapy."

Robin listened without movement or comment, allowing Martin to continue speaking.

"Those physical scars...they're the least of what I went through. And then, a year after they finally gave up and threw me out, they died. I hadn't spoken to them since they made me leave. I was shocked when the lawyers contacted me, and I realized that they hadn't changed their wills. And I'm never going to be able to ask them if they left them as they were on purpose, or if it was just that they never got around to changing them. We're never going to reconcile...it's never going to be anything but what it was, and it was a nightmare. It was parents torturing their child and believing themselves righteous for doing so."

He turned, so he was facing Robin again, the ruin of his back hidden away from Robin's line of vision. "What I'm saying is humans aren't safe. So what makes vampires more frightening than them?" Martin gave a huff of humorless laughter. "Sorry. That whole tragic backstory—heh, *backstory*—is pretty heavy stuff for a first date, I guess. But then again, you're a vampire who's made me come without letting me return the favor, so maybe we're even."

"Is that important to you? That I feel pleasure, too?"

"Of course it is. If I only cared about myself, why bother dating someone else in the first place?"

Robin looked down, expression shy but without any hint of a blush: the same as Martin had seen him look before.

"Not this time, I'd need..." he said to Martin quietly. He sounded embarrassed. "I'd need to drink more of your blood to be able to get hard. I don't have enough of my own to do it."

The confession opened up an entire universe of further questions that Martin wanted to ask. Now his initial surprise was beginning to fade, genuine fascination was taking its place.

But there would be other chances to ask Robin about all those things. For now, Martin was feeling extremely tired. It had been a long day by any definition. He was glad it was one of his days off tomorrow; there was no way he'd be bright-eyed and chipper first thing in the morning, not after staying up into the small hours like some teenager who could bounce back without consequences after a night out.

"I think it is well and truly time for me to get some sleep," Martin said, his point proven by the wide yawn that punctuated the declaration.

Robin looked over toward the door, scrubbing at the back of his neck with one hand in a nervous gesture. "I guess I should—"

"You're more than welcome to stay," Martin assured him. "I'd like you to stay."

Robin hesitated, pressing his lips together, clearly conflicted about the offer. Then he nodded, taking off his clothes and joining Martin in the bed. They negotiated the shared space awkwardly for a few moments, trying to work out how they best fit together, before settling down with Robin curled against Martin's back, one arm resting on his waist.

Robin's breath didn't feel like breath against Martin's skin; there was no dampness or warmth to it. It was like a rhythmic puff of air brushing his shoulder blade, nothing more. His solidity was real enough, though, even without temperature. Martin fell asleep quickly.

He woke up cold, which he soon realized was because the window in his bedroom had been left ajar and unlocked. Shivering, Martin climbed out of bed. He wrapped the blanket around his shoulders as he shuffled over and closed the pane. Since he was awake, he decided he might as well get up properly.

He wasn't surprised that Robin was nowhere to be seen. Martin had already guessed that the guy wasn't exactly the hang-around-for-coffee-and-eggs type.

Martin thought back to all the thrown-out cups he'd watched Robin buy and then fail to drink on his visits to The Warm Taste. Was Robin even capable of eating or drinking ordinary food? And, if not, had that all been an elaborate, completely meaningless charade to get close to Martin?

He didn't think so. That might be what Robin thought the sole reason was, but Martin suspected his true motivation had been a slightly broader one, even if Robin hadn't known it consciously. Nobody could thrive in isolation. Everyone needed connection to others, even if it was as tenuous as sharing space with them inside a bustling coffee shop during the evenings.

As Martin walked into the living room, he saw that his bedroom window hadn't been an isolated incident: every other window, and every door, in his house was unlocked and slightly ajar—not enough that anyone outside of the building would immediately see, but enough that Martin couldn't fail to notice.

Nora, seeing he was awake, jumped down from where she'd been sleeping on the sofa. "Jumped" might have been giving her more credit than was due; the movement was more like lazily allowing gravity to pull her legs toward the floor. She stumbled over to him with a wide doggy yawn that Martin shouldn't have found nearly as endearing as he did.

"You're the most pathetic guard dog in the world," he told her in a dry voice, scratching her between her ears. "Thanks for that."

Nora yipped happily.

There was a note on his table; the handwriting extremely neat, the script old-fashioned.

It's a very dangerous thing, to love a vampire, Robin had written. *Think about all the things you're risking.*

"Glad to see he isn't melodramatic, then," Martin said flatly, resisting the urge to sigh. It had been a long time since he'd been with anyone; trust him to wind up with the guy with a literally inhuman pile of issues.

He went around the house, locking all the opened entry points that Robin had so helpfully provided. Then, since he was awake and chilly already, he dressed and put on a coat and then took Nora out for a morning walk.

Chapter Three

Robin

The coffee shop, in addition to its living, human good points, turned out to be an excellent place to sit and read. That was probably what made it so popular with students who needed to learn or write—despite the general hubbub of background noise, The Warm Taste had such a friendly, calming vibe that even at its busiest and loudest it was still a place where it was easy to relax and concentrate.

Robin, seated at one of the tables most distant from the counter, turned to the next page of a scuffed paperback called *Oscar's Books: A Journey Around the Library of Oscar Wilde*, which he'd stolen from a shelf in Martin's house. Martin had a lot of books, on topics so eclectic that it was almost as if he'd chosen them at random, based on a momentary interest in the subject.

It was yet another way in which Robin found him unfathomable. How someone could have so much enthusiasm and fascination for so many different topics was a complete mystery to Robin, who found the very thought of caring about even his most immediate concerns exhausting.

The book was still in quite a readable state, despite the secondhand wear and tear on the pages and cover. It was a long time since Robin had read anything. He'd loved novels when he was alive; all his money had gone on acquiring as many as he could afford. There had been times when he'd lived on cups of tea and cigarettes, forgoing even bread and cheese in favor of buying just a few more books that week.

But that had been a long, long time ago. Now he didn't read at all. He couldn't engage with the worlds that authors crafted for him. Fiction meant work, thought, imagination. Robin didn't have it in him to manage any of those, not anymore.

Even the book on Wilde's library, non-fiction and biographical as it was, pushed Robin far outside the wordless comfort zone he'd been in for so long.

The thought made a crooked smile pull at one corner of his mouth. A comfort zone without the least bit of comfort within it. That described his life quite well.

Sarah's daughter, Polly, was seated at the table she had declared as permanently her own. She had her phone in her hands and was tapping away furiously at it, her thumbs moving up and down the sides of the screen to the rhythm of a tinny pop song quietly chiming out of the phone's speaker. The lyrics weren't in English; Robin knew a number of other languages, but this wasn't any of the ones he knew. Based on the small amount of knowledge Robin had about modern popular culture, he guessed the most likely candidate was Japanese.

The song ended with a few tones that suggested the latest round of the game had ended in failure, and Polly slumped forward, burying her face between her outstretched arms on the tabletop with a groan.

"I hate this game," she complained in a petulant voice, addressing nobody in particular. After another few seconds of bent-over misery, she sat up and tapped at the phone again, restarting the song and resuming her previous quick-fire pace.

Her mercurial moods, swinging from despair to determination in a matter of moments, reminded Robin of how his sisters had faced the world. They'd all shared that same tendency, although in most other ways they hadn't been much like Polly at all.

Robin hadn't thought of them in almost as long as it had been since he stopped reading.

As far as elements of the living world went, Robin's family had been an even harder habit to rid himself of than his old infatuation with the written word. He'd remained interested in their lives long after his own had ended.

The first time Robin had seen Polly, he'd wondered if she was a vampire, too. She'd seemed to fit all the criteria: her appearance made her seem younger than her real age, and she had a greedy, possessive streak to her personality. She was extremely pretty, but the prettiness had an edge of sickliness and frailty to it that made it seem consumptive and eerie; her eyes slightly too bright, her skin so pale that the veins of her wrists were visible through the slightly translucent white there.

But Robin had been mistaken. Polly was exactly as she appeared to be: a child prone to illness and stunted by years of bad health, her fractious personality the result of helpless rage against constant sickness.

Robin supposed he was glad about that. Glad she was alive. He would never wish existence as a vampire on anyone, especially not a child. But. Still. It had been a very long time since he'd known anyone like him. It would have been...

But no. It was better not to even think about what might have been. Things were as they were. There was no point in wishing otherwise.

"Ugh!" Polly, sounding deeply annoyed, tossed the phone onto the table. "I had a twenty-five-note combo and the battery died. Perfect. Just perfect."

One of the other patrons, a red-haired student with a stature he hadn't quite yet learned to pilot gracefully, approached Polly's table and asked her a question. Robin could have listened to what he was saying by paying close attention but didn't bother.

Preternaturally sharp senses were somewhat wasted on Robin, all told. He didn't engage with the world around him even to the degree that ordinary humans did, let alone seek to make use of the natural precision of a vampire's hunting tools: hearing, smell, sight, taste, strength.

Polly's reply to the redheaded student's question was to pick up her discarded phone and turn it upside-down, showing him something on the short, narrow edge of the device's base. He nodded and went back to his own table, where after a minute's rummaging, he removed a long cable and a hefty-looking rectangular object from his messenger bag. He returned to Polly's table, handing over the portable charger with a helpful, shy smile.

She smiled back and plugged in her phone, firing up the game again as soon as it had enough battery to run. The young man returned to his own table and to his studies. His momentary look of satisfaction at having solved Polly's dilemma was soon replaced by an expression of exhausted stress.

Robin had long ago ceased to be surprised when days and weeks passed rapidly without his notice, so it didn't shock him to realize, as he glanced around the room, that the other patrons who were engaged in studies all had similar expressions to the one the young man's face now wore. The semester was in full swing, then, fraying their young confidence.

Robin watched the red-haired student as he worked. It made him remember another time and place, long ago and far away, when his older brother had sat in much the same posture. Reading and writing late into the night, kept from the opportunities of university by obligations on their family's farm but in love with knowledge nonetheless, and determined to know as much about everything as he could.

Now, Robin thought—no, now Robin knew—he had been foolish to bother. Once Robin's brother had been killed, that wonderful, brilliant brain of his had been no different from any other cooling meat. Thoughts and dreams were meaningless, as invisible as a clever vampire. They had no useful, tangible role in the world.

He wondered if the young man bent over his books in the coffee shop knew that. Robin thought he might, in the pale and distant way that people often knew the futility at the bottom of their labors. There was some telltale element in the set of his face and body; an existential numbness that Robin recognized simply because its identical twin had so long lived in his own heart.

This was a person who knew how little anything mattered, or could ever matter.

As Robin sat, watching someone other than Martin for the first time since he'd first visited The Warm Taste, Sarah approached the book-strewn table, a large coffee cup in her hand.

"As thanks for saving us all," Sarah explained, gesturing toward Polly's small form, which was still attached to the handheld game with single-minded focus. "I'd try to say she's not usually that overdramatic, but I'm starting to think I screwed up somewhere with the parenting."

"No, no." The student laughed, shaking his head. "I was the same. That's how I know to carry different cords and a recharged battery—my babysitter always had a couple of spares, or a power pack, in her purse just in case. Now I'm the one who babysits, I know to always do the same. So it's no big deal or anything. Not that I'm gonna turn down the free coffee, though."

Sarah looked pleased. "Glad to hear it."

As Sarah walked away, a photograph in one of the textbooks on the young man's table caught Robin's eye. It was of William Haines, a movie star who'd been popular not long after Robin had become a vampire.

Robin had spent a lot of time at the cinema in those first years. Watching the slightly surreal flicker of silent movies was easier for him than trying to pretend that he still had a place in the real, colorful world beyond the walls of the darkened theatre, where the living were.

He found himself leaning over, addressing the young man. "What're you studying?"

"I'm supposed to be writing a presentation on an important example of how LGBTQ people have been oppressed and subjugated," the student answered before even looking up from his work. "I'm doing cultural studies, and one of my lecturers heard some genius in the class talking about how there's no sexuality or gender oppression anymore, because there's marriage equality now and a trans woman was on the front of *Vanity Fair*. So the lecturer decided we all needed a history lesson to cure us of some of our ignorance, and then she's going to make us study modern-day oppressions next so we don't think it's all over now. I'm Ben, by the way." Looking up at Robin, he grinned and held out a hand.

"Robin," Robin replied, shaking the hand with his own. "So you're writing on William Haines?"

Ben nodded. "Yeah. You've heard of him?"

"I've seen some of his movies, but that's all I know."

"He got thrown out of Hollywood for choosing his real husband over a fake wife. I mean, not his real-real husband. They didn't marry or anything. Nobody had any idea that two men getting married would ever be something that happened, not at all. Nobody ever knew to want it; it was so outside the realms of what people dreamed of having the chance to do. But...I feel like the other guy was his real husband all the same—they were together from the moment they met until one of them died, you know? How many couples manage that, honestly? They loved each other so much that when Haines died, his husband couldn't bear the thought of living without him and overdosed on sleeping pills very soon after, explaining in his suicide note that the loneliness of being without Haines was the reason for his own death."

"So being loyal to his lover ruined his life?" Robin asked. "They were the Romeo and Juliet of the silent era?" He wasn't surprised to hear that the whole thing had ended in disaster. In Robin's experience, there wasn't truly such a thing as happy endings, not even for movie stars from golden Hollywood.

"Oh, no, he actually had it great after he left the movie business," Ben assured him. "He started an interior design company that's still going even now and lived to a ripe old age. They were together fifty years. It was a fairy tale, not a tragedy. So it's not all that great as an example, maybe, even though he did have to give up being a movie star."

Ben frowned, sighing. "This whole assignment is a depressing disaster. I could strangle the ignorant idiot who mouthed off about marriage equality, honestly. They've doubled my workload." He took a long drink of the free coffee Sarah had given him, despite the fact that it must have been quite cool by that stage. "I'm basically at a loss."

Robin considered the dilemma for a long moment. "You could do it on the two women who got married in Spain in 1901," he suggested. "They were a couple, and lived together, but decided they wanted it acknowledged in the eyes of the church."

"I've never heard of them. Did they manage it? How on earth would they, that far back?"

"Yes, they did. First they pretended to have a huge fight and 'broke up,' and one of them moved away," Robin told Ben. "Then she came back, having assumed the identity of a cousin she'd had who had died in a shipwreck. She'd even been baptized under her new male name. The two of them got married and started living as husband and wife, but their neighbors worked out what was happening and reported them. There was only so much that anybody could ignore, and trying to be legitimate in the eyes of the church was clearly overstepping that invisible line. They were fired from their jobs, lost their home, and had to go on the run, fleeing the authorities while the press denounced them. During their escape they boarded a boat, and nobody knows what happened to them after that."

"Holy shit."

"Not exactly a happy ending making furniture, no."

"I think this would be perfect for my assignment. Do you remember their names?"

Robin shook his head. "Sorry, no. But you should be able to find out more online without much trouble."

Ben nodded in agreement, scribbling down notes. "Yeah, I'll look it up when I get home. Thanks."

"No problem." Robin managed another small smile. He'd approximated more human facial expressions in this one conversation than he'd had in the last century put together, probably, not counting interactions with Martin. "Glad I could help. It's not up there with magical problem-solving babysitter powers, but I hope it was at least a bit useful."

Ben laughed. "Anyone can be a good babysitter. It's no big skill."

"Are you joking? Nobody is deluded enough to sincerely think babysitting is easy, are they? You can't be serious."

"Have you ever actually done it? It's not a big deal, honestly."

"Well, no, I haven't," Robin admitted. "But even the thought of it is pretty damn intimidating. And while I've never been a babysitter, I did work as a translator in Paris for tourists, which was the same thing in some ways."

"That's pretty mean about tourists, man."

"No, no," Robin protested. "I didn't mean it that way. I meant because you're the one they have to trust completely, from the moment you take charge of them. Their wellbeing is in your hands. You're the ambassador between them and the wider world. It's a responsibility. It's intimidating."

"Oh, I get it." Nodding, Ben shifted to face Robin more directly. "That must have been cool, though. Living in France."

Robin shrugged. "It was okay. The city's wonderful; don't get me wrong or anything. It's just that everyone's so intense about Paris, you know? Like, super crazy intense about it. Parisians are assholes about it; tourists are nuts about it. Did you know that there's a hotline specifically for Japanese travelers suffering a shock of depression after arriving in Paris and getting disillusioned about it?"

"There should be more metropolis-related mental health services, in my opinion," Ben declared. "Ever been to LA? That place is a sprawling, polluted case of existential despair right there."

Robin's mouth twitched into a grin. "I've heard that's the case. Hm...oh, I know. If you want to go into the psychotic realms, try Pyongyang. Emotional logic, the things you see—it genuinely does get to feeling like your thoughts and senses can't be trusted anymore."

"Oh, well, I can't top that." Ben shrugged. "All the places I've been are low-grade panic disorders at best. "

The two of them continued talking, their shared fatalistic sense of humor winding them through descriptions of cities they'd visited and jobs they'd had. Eventually, Robin began to feel guilty at the amount of Ben's time he was taking up, which was a new and rare experience, since vampires were naturally parasitic when it came to humans. Taking without consideration of how that impacted on those they were taking from was what made a vampire—well, a vampire.

Then again, he'd always made sure that Martin had a nutritious meal after being fed from. Robin's brain was probably defective in some fundamental way. The tendency to give at least a small amount of a damn was like a bad habit he didn't know how to break.

After saying good-bye and leaving Ben to his studies, Robin stood up and went over to where Martin was steaming a jug of milk.

"I'm going home now. I'll catch up with you in a couple of nights, all right? I'll text you."

"I look forward to it," Martin replied, and the warmth in his voice made Robin want to get his phone out and write said text immediately, even before leaving The Warm Taste at all.

The sky outside was slightly overcast, obscuring the majority of the stars. A few of the brightest and nearest shone through, however—enough to serve as a reminder of how limitless reality was.

For the first time in his long, long memory, Robin could feel himself looking forward to the future as he walked home, genuinely smiling.

Chapter Four

Martin

The text from Robin came a few nights later, and Martin tried to pretend that he was a laid-back, casual guy who had in no way been compulsively checking his phone for the message's arrival. He didn't convince even himself, though. He liked Robin a lot and was eager to spend more time with him.

They arranged to meet up at Martin's house and decide what to do for an outing once Robin arrived. Robin was forty minutes late, which gave Martin another opportunity to pretend—this time that he was laid-back and casual and paying no attention to the clock. It was about as convincing as pretending he wasn't checking his phone had been.

When Robin did arrive, the pair of them kissed hello in Martin's doorway, doing their best to ignore the small dog anxiously yelling at Robin for attention.

"What do you want to do tonight?" Martin asked. "I've tried my hardest to think of dates I could take you on, but we've already done the movies. Restaurants for a nice dinner aren't an option, since I assume you don't need food as well as blood—wait, should I assume that? Can you eat food? Do you want to go out to dinner?"

Robin gave him a lazy, lascivious smile, eyelids dropping low enough that his lashes were a dark fan, alluring against the pallor of his skin. "We don't need to go out. If we stay in, I can have you for dinner."

Martin resisted the urge to roll his eyes. He liked hanging out with Robin, but as soon as he tried to do anything nice for the guy, Robin slipped into a strange superficiality, full of stilted attempts at being seductive.

Martin wasn't into it at all, but going through the mannered motions seemed to put Robin at ease, so he let it slide.

"We could go to the college campus," Robin suggested, momentarily forgetting to be the clichéd version of an alluring, attractive vampire. "Just walk around. That obviously works for the hundreds of student couples who hang around there, right?"

"Sounds good to me."

☆☆☆

The huge university library had a scattering of students in it, working on laptops or scribbling in notebooks; heads bowed over their work or faces raised, gazes fixed on the middle distance as complex thoughts untangled slowly inside their skulls.

They were like a quieter variety of the same sort of kids Martin had coming into the coffee shop every night of the week. The venue of choice was different, but the goal was the same: to create work that made sense, and to learn enough to convince others that they knew what they were talking about.

Martin had heard naysayers complain that college didn't prepare kids for the real world, but in his opinion—as someone who hadn't gone to college, but who hopefully knew at least a little bit about the real world—it seemed like pretty good training, really. Adulthood wasn't much more than striving to make sense and bullshitting people into thinking you knew more than you did.

The people against college got too caught up in the content of the things that students learned about there, declaring it useless or without common application, instead of paying attention to the fact that what students were gaining was an understanding of how to apply method. Provided the method got learned, the content was just window dressing, really. Graduates could apply what they'd learn about method to whatever they did next, instead of having to flail around like Martin had.

He'd known from a young age that he wanted to be nurturing, nourishing, and helpful for those around him. He hadn't known that those dreams would take the form of owning The Warm Taste, or taking care of a useless little dog, or dating a vampire who was the emotional equivalent of a tire fire, until those things had turned up. His content had been there, but the method had been cobbled together as he went along, because he'd never been taught how to have one.

Then again, he'd never gone to college, so what did he really know about any of that stuff?

The only word to describe how Martin felt about the library was stunned. Shelf after shelf was crammed from floor to ceiling with books; old hardcovers and glossy new volumes. And the building was seven stories tall. And it was only one of several libraries on campus. Stunned barely covered it.

He picked a shelf at random, boggling at the esoteric and fascinating titles presented to him. "This place makes me wish I had enough time to read everything, you know?"

"I suppose," Robin replied, though his tone was doubtful. "More time doesn't necessarily mean time well used, though. It's easier to put things off when you've got forever."

Martin didn't know what to say about that, so he took Robin's hand in his own and offered a reassuring squeeze.

Robin stood slightly tiptoed and Martin bent down, the two of them meeting in the space between with a slow press of mouth to mouth. The kiss began gently and deepened quickly, Martin licking into Robin's mouth and rucking his shirt up slightly, then running a hand over the smooth, soft skin just above his hip.

47

That Robin had no body temperature save for that of the air around them was something Martin was still struggling to get used to, but there were senses other than temperature that touch could satisfy. The small, needy whimpers that Robin made, as quiet as he could force himself to be in the silent space, were extremely gratifying for Martin. That he could drive Robin crazy, when Robin's self-control was so strictly kept in check, was like winning a prize, or cracking a code.

"I want to hear so many sounds from you," Martin murmured quietly into Robin's mouth. "I want to tease a hundred moans out of you."

"Probably not the best idea, in a library," Robin teased.

"Maybe we should go back to my place, then."

"That's what I was saying from the start." The lascivious smile that Robin wore like a well-rehearsed mask slipped back into place. This time, its appearance made Martin even more determined to wring honest, unbridled reactions from Robin later; reactions Robin couldn't hold back. That Robin's honest thoughts and feelings were so elusive made them worth working even harder to reveal.

They left the library and walked back through the sprawling campus, which was lit with streetlamps along its pretty, paved pathways; the sides of the pathways lined with occasional benches. It was a very inviting place, the kind that Martin could imagine its students having very fond memories of after they left it for the wider world.

"It's novel for me, being here," Martin admitted. "I never went to college myself. I feel a little bit like I'm an imposter, being here now, even though we're just walking around."

"I didn't, either. Go to college, I mean," Robin said. He bit his lip, but no extra bloom of color chased the pressure. "I know what you mean about feeling like an imposter, too."

Martin felt a brief moment of regret for having phrased it like that. Of course Robin would find a way to take an idle comment about being at a school they'd never gone to and find the lonely, wider metaphor inside it.

Robin's gloomy tendencies were simultaneously slightly amusing and strongly upsetting, in Martin's opinion. They were amusing because they reminded him of so many of the people he'd seen in The Warm Taste over the years; the black-clad poets and sad-eyed artists, all of them under the impression that sensitivity and misery had to go hand in hand. He could never meet one of that tribe without feeling a vague desire to take them to the dog park with Nora and a Frisbee for a few hours, just to see how long they'd hold out before letting a little of the world's bright happiness in alongside their sorrow.

The sadness was much more upsetting than it was funny, though. Unexpected vampirism aside, Martin felt as if he'd been pretty much on the money with his first assessments of what Robin was like: lonely, socially awkward, and massively depressed. And while all of those things could be joked about by Robin, on the rare occasions that he revealed he had a sense of humor at all, they weren't things that Martin could ever find funny on his behalf. They were terrible, isolating things, and who knew how long Robin had been trapped by them?

It wasn't a long walk back to Martin's home from the college. He'd deliberately positioned The Warm Taste in the general radius of where students were likely to gather, and from there it had made sense to choose a house that was close enough to his business that he could easily get to and from work on foot.

While Martin was getting his keys out and unlocking the front door, Robin reached out and pressed a palm against Martin's half-hard cock, making a pleased sound.

"I can't wait to get my mouth on that," he purred. Martin

shook his head.

"We're not having a remake of last time, where all we do is just you giving me a blow job."

Robin made a faux-offended noise of protest. "Excuse me; there was nothing *just* about that blow job."

"True," Martin conceded, getting the door open and navigating around the instantly present Nora as she noisily got underfoot.

He gave her a bowl of food and refreshed her water so that she'd be occupied for long enough for them to make it to the bedroom without having to hear pitiful whining from the other side of it when they shut the door.

"Do you need to bite me first so that you can—" Martin started to ask, wondering if there was any non-awkward, non-ridiculous-sounding way to ask a lover if they needed a drink of blood before they could get erect.

Obviously, Robin considered avoiding the question completely to be the most preferable way of answering. He shook his head, giving Martin another of those shallow, sexy smiles. "It's fine. There's other things I want to do instead. Do you have lubricant?"

Martin nodded, retrieving the tube from a shelf in his closet and tossing it onto the bed.

Stripping each other of clothing turned into a mess of fumbling and almost falling over, which wound up making them both snort with laughter.

"We'll never get naked, at this rate," Robin said. "It's a sad fate, but we'll have to be resigned to it."

His tone was so long-suffering and angelic that Martin could hardly stand how cute he was, which in turn made Martin want to laugh even more. "I'm probably not meant to be finding a vampire that I'm about to have sex with cute, am I? It's probably all meant to be more Gothic and torrid than we're managing."

Robin snorted with laughter again. "You are, quite literally, the least Gothic and torrid person I have ever met, and you bring out the least Gothic and torrid in me."

"Hey, it's not me that's meant to be bringing that vibe with me. You're the one letting your side down. Though that's not completely true; you do have that capital-R Romantic thing going, I guess. You've got intense eyes, and I bet you've read Edgar Allen Poe—"

"Guilty."

"And Goethe—"

"Guilty again."

"And Mary Shelley's *Frankenstein*—"

"Guilty the third time."

"And John Polidori's *The Vampyre*—"

"Okay, okay, yes, I am a cliché," Robin cut him off with smile. "I sat in candlelit rooms and read poetry. Now shut up and touch me."

"Well, that's not very romantic of you, I gotta say."

"I just told you that you bring out the least Gothic and torrid parts of me, didn't I?" retorted Robin.

It was a flippant reply, but Martin thought there might be a degree of truth to it. Robin seemed sometimes to be able to forget himself, and the cold, blank sadness that pervaded his movements and speech, when he was with Martin. Not completely, of course, but a little.

They eventually, finally got themselves divested of clothing and tumbled naked onto Martin's bed. Martin looked down at Robin, who lay on his back staring up, and the lighthearted mood of minutes earlier abruptly turned darker and hotter.

They kissed again, deeply and slowly, as Martin folded one of Robin's legs up until the knee was level with their shoulders. "Is

51

that all right?"

"Yes, it's fine. Hurry up," Robin answered. Martin reached down between them, his hand seeking out Robin's entrance and rubbing slow, light circles with one finger.

"You need to put lube on that, you know," Robin offered, obviously trying for flippancy but falling short, betrayed by the hitch in his voice and the way he was trying to angle his body closer to Martin's finger.

"Don't be so impatient," Martin hushed him. He was so hard that it was a little uncomfortable, but he just shifted his position slightly and refocused his attention on Robin.

He stroked Robin with soft touches, adding lube so that he could start alternating the slow circles with shallow pushes inside—just enough to tease the sensitive nerves, everything careful and delicate and tender.

Robin had gone quiet. He didn't tease Martin with any more wisecracks, or say anything else at all. His eyes were squeezed shut, as if he was enduring something uncomfortable, or even painful.

Martin slid two fingers into Robin the next time, deeper than any of the previous touches. That earned a sigh from Robin, and his eyes opened again to stare up at Martin, the pupils so huge and dark that there was only the thinnest ring of blue around them.

"Tell me how that feels," Martin said. Robin didn't reply; his body squeezing around Martin's fingers.

Martin bent his head low, to lick at Robin's nipple. Robin's back arched at the touch, chasing it as Martin pulled back, want and need becoming increasingly obvious in his expression. Martin pressed his other hand to Robin's heaving chest, pinning him down gently, steadying him in place. Tethering him to the world.

Even as he was clearly aching with the need for more, Robin remained silent.

"Please," Martin said in a rough whisper. "I want to hear you. I need to know you're good. You have to tell me when it feels good."

Robin raised his eyebrows in surprise, as if he was shocked that Martin would wonder at such a thing. His body clenched around Martin's fingers greedily, but Martin remained still.

"I...like controlling myself," Robin said slowly, obviously realizing that Martin wouldn't continue until he got a reply. "Letting go...making noise, that's difficult for me. But I'll...I'll try."

Martin smiled at him, leaning over his body to kiss his lips. "I know you can do it."

Martin resumed working Robin open, stretching his hole wide with slow, careful pushes of his fingers. He could feel the preternatural strength that permeated every part of Robin's body, and the way Robin stayed open and welcoming for him despite that.

As Martin moved his mouth down from Robin's, sucking gently at Robin's jaw and throat, Robin's breaths grew harsh. Martin added a third finger and that harsh breathing stuttered with a small gulping sound, and then another.

"Come on," Martin coaxed. "I know you can give me more than that."

He teased his fingertip over Robin's prostate lightly. Robin choked back a whimper.

"Let it out."

"Harder," Robin gasped, trying to fuck himself down onto Martin's hand. Martin stilled again.

"That's better," he told Robin, fixing his mouth around one of Robin's nipples and sucking lightly. Robin's gasp was a quiet wail, his body trying once again to arch up.

"More, more, harder, please, bite it," he pleaded in a strained voice, his body tight like a vise around Martin's slick fingers, chest straining up under Martin's mouth.

Martin moved away just enough to speak, his lips and breath ghosting against the pebbled flesh of Robin's nipple with each word. "No, not this time."

Robin whined, trembling. Martin moved up his body again, capturing Robin in a kiss simultaneously with easing his hand back from where his fingers had been inside Robin's body. Robin whined again, louder this time, the sound muffled by the fit of their mouths against each other.

It was obvious that Robin couldn't cope with tenderness, perhaps to the point of genuine distress. He knew how to handle being hurt, but not how to handle this. It made Martin's own breath catch on a lump in his throat, sorrow on Robin's behalf making his eyes sting.

Martin reached up with his clean hand and cupped Robin's face as gently as he could, keeping their gazes locked as he aligned their bodies so that his cock was against Robin's open, readied hole and then pushed into Robin for the first time. It earned another soft wail out of Robin, followed by a string of the small gulping sounds.

Martin shushed him softly. "It's okay. Just let it feel good. It's all right."

Robin clung to Martin's arms, shuddering as Martin pulled back and pushed in again, slowly and deliberately, and then did it again.

"How are you doing?" Martin asked, though he could tell easily enough by now how Robin was doing. Robin was wrecked.

"Feels...feels good," Robin managed to answer. "I can't...fuck, fuck, Martin, I can't, oh..." A bitten-off sob cracked his words apart.

Tears slipped from the corners of Robin's eyes as he arched his whole body like a bow, head tipping back and mouth opening.

He was murmuring to himself, the words swinging from English to German to French to others that Martin didn't recognize.

Martin kept his steady, even pace throughout, every thrust causing Robin to make another hiccupping sound, making his hands splay and clutch erratically against Martin's biceps. He was shivering, moaning, sighing.

"You can come, Robin. I've got you," Martin whispered.

Robin shoved his face into the crook of Martin's shoulder, not to bite but to muffle a scream that wrenched free as he shivered through his climax, clinging onto Martin for dear life. The feel of Robin's body tightening around him was enough to send Martin over the brink, as well; he'd been holding back, ignoring his own pleasure in favor of focusing on ensuring that Robin felt as good as possible.

It seemed to take a very long time for the shivery aftershocks of pleasure to pass, and by the time they did, Martin wanted nothing more than to fall into a long, deep sleep. Instead, he rubbed small, light circles onto Robin's back; little soothing animal touches to help ground him as his heaving, gulping breaths calmed back down to regular inhales and exhales.

Robin started at Martin, as if trying to comprehend something that made no sense whatsoever. Martin gave him a slow, tender kiss and then moved back.

"You okay?" Martin asked, worried for one long moment that he'd pushed Robin too far outside his comfort zone. And then Robin's face lit up with a bright, uncomplicated smile.

It was such a genuine look of happiness that Martin's heart flipped over at the sight of it, his stomach momentarily filled with that butterfly-feeling he could remember from when he was young; the sensation of utter and absolute infatuation with another person.

It struck him as incredibly sad that Robin, so reserved and

occasionally downright dour, seemed so reluctant to have anything straightforwardly happy in his life, any tenderness or joy. He seemed so certain that to invite those emotions in was to bring about some inevitable doom that had been waiting, invisible and malevolent, to steal whatever small good things Robin might manage to find.

But if anything was the true indicator of doom, it was that brilliant, happy smile on Robin's face. Martin could feel it in the dizzy swoop of his own heart. He was doomed, doomed, doomed. Nobody could look at Robin's face in that moment, with its open joy, and not be irrevocably, inevitably bound to him, no matter what.

The thought made Martin grin, and then laugh aloud. He kissed Robin's lovely face, with its cool, pale skin and delightful sunshine smile.

They eventually fell asleep curled against each other, and Martin could hardly believe Robin would trust him like that— would be so vulnerable and defenseless in Martin's presence. It felt like a valuable gift.

Chapter Five

Robin

The insistent ringing of his mobile telephone woke him. Robin hated the thing; he'd only bought it because he'd realized that his not owning one was becoming remarkable to other people. In the interest of blending in, which was above all other concerns, Robin had bought himself a cellphone.

And he loathed it, loathed owning it. As soon as a device was put on the market which allowed for texting but not for telephone calls, he was trading his phone in for one immediately. Face-to-face interaction was bad enough; on the telephone people expected immediate replies to questions. It was as if the world had devised the form of communication which most resembled Robin's worst nightmare, and made it standard.

When the sheer force of his hatred failed to melt the small plastic rectangle, Robin reached a hand out from under the covers and groped at the pile of discarded clothes beside the bed. He retrieved the phone from the pocket of his jeans.

Putting it to his ear, he pulled the blankets over his head, hoping that they would somehow cut off reception and end the call before it began. "Hello?"

"Mr. St John? This is Lauren Edwards, from Executive Security Holdings."

Robin always thought of Lauren's voice as glossy, the same perfect-lacquer scarlet as her nails and lips perhaps. She'd become his personal account advisor when he'd done one of the periodic transfers of his accounts from one banking corporation to another, something he did in order to avoid developing a long-term relationship with any single one of them.

Unfortunately, it seemed that "relationship" was the watchword of doing business these days. Lauren sent him Christmas cards, for crying out loud. And, even more bafflingly, she clearly made a concentrated effort to sound friendly and personable whenever she spoke to him on the telephone, no matter how obvious Robin made it that he didn't like—not to mention, wasn't any good at—pleasantries, and wanted all communication to be as brief and to the point as it could possibly be.

Outside his blanket cocoon, Robin could hear the small sounds of Martin drawing the window shades closed, making the room sunless and comfortable. Robin stayed under the bedding anyway. Hopefully he could get rid of Lauren quickly, and they could go back to sleep.

"Your coworkers must really dislike you," Robin said, his usual carefully unremarkable persona under strain from the annoyance of being woken up. "Since you always get stuck with the task of calling me."

"It's standard procedure, Mr. St John," Lauren told him in her bright, glossy voice. "Accounts of your size always have a personal staff liaison who handles all transactions and enquiries. I'm yours."

"I know, I know," Robin grumbled. "So what is it that you've called me about? I haven't made any transactions recently, or enquiries for that matter."

"There's been some activity on your account from international locations. Executive Security Holdings just wanted to let you know we've stopped all attempted withdrawals and are committed to protecting your assets from fraud and theft."

Robin had to stop himself from laughing. "Assuming that the situation actually happened, and isn't just Executive Security Holdings trying to make itself look heroic and important, then you needn't have bothered. I don't care if thieves take it. In fact, they're welcome to it; they clearly worked for it, and it isn't like I'm doing anything with it."

Lauren's tone didn't falter for a second. Robin hoped the bank was paying her an enormous amount of money to deal with his cranky bullshit. "Just letting you know, sir. Have a good day."

Denied the old-fashioned pleasure of physically putting down a receiver in order to end the call, Robin hit the button and tossed the phone back down toward his clothing.

"You have a really old phone," Martin remarked, joining Robin inside the small, dark space beneath the covers.

"Can't use the ones that are only touch screens," Robin explained. "They don't react to my fingers and thumbs often enough, because of the temperature. It annoyed me."

"There are those specially made pens you can get, to use on the screens. You could buy one of those."

"That would annoy me, too."

Martin chuckled. "Everything annoys you. I don't know how you'd even notice a difference."

"You have a point." Robin shuffled over on the bed until their bodies were flush, the warmth of Martin's body so strong and bright against Robin's own flesh that he couldn't help but curl against him happily, as if he could absorb that heat through simple touch.

They stayed like that, in the warm dark, without saying a word, for some time. Then Martin spoke, his hand stroking through Robin's hair as he did.

"You know, it's possibly not the greatest idea in the world to be that careless with money," he said.

Robin shrugged, as much as he could without moving out of Martin's arms. "You're just the same, though. You let yours just sit there, too."

Martin didn't comment on the fact that Robin clearly knew all about Martin's own personal finances. "That's not true. I opened The Warm Taste, didn't I? I use my money when I need it. I'm just waiting until there's something else I need the rest for."

"Yeah, well, there's never anything I need mine for, so a bunch of Nigerian hackers might as well take it."

Martin made a disapproving noise, but didn't say anything. Robin ignored the noise. Let Martin think whatever he liked; Robin didn't care.

A few minutes later Martin moved in closer, pressing a soft kiss to Robin's mouth. Robin kissed back by reflex, licking at Martin's lips, letting his teeth nip against the vulnerable skin. Martin gave a happy-sounding hum, opening to the insistence of Robin's tongue and letting him inside; the two lost in one another for a long, dreamlike stretch of time in the heated dark of their little world beneath the covers.

Robin wasn't sure that he could handle another round of Martin's style of sex, not so soon after last time anyway. The intensity of it, even in memory, made him tremble.

He was still slick and open from the night before, so all it took was working Martin's length into hardness with his hand, then straddling his body and sliding into place atop him, filled to the hilt. Robin had to hold back a groan at how good it felt; he tried to remember why he'd thought this way would be a less intense experience.

The covers had become more of a hindrance than a novelty, so Robin shrugged them off and let them slide away off the side of the bed.

"You feel so good, you know that?" Martin asked him, resting both hands on Robin's hips as they moved together. "You make me want to spend the rest of my life right here, fucking you."

"Everyone's going to think you're a sugar daddy, when you're seventy and I still look eighteen," Robin teased him. "Will that bother you?"

"Ask me again when I'm seventy," Martin replied, making Robin laugh.

He didn't know quite how to handle the blossoming mutual power he could feel himself sharing with Martin. They were willingly trading vulnerability, each giving the other the ability to cause great harm. Trust of any kind came hard to Robin, especially a trust that demanded such total surrender to another person. His instincts urged him to gain dominance, to take charge of the situation and protect himself. Robin felt as if he could handle pretty much anything, so long as he was the one in control.

Now that he only had control equal to the amount he was willing to relinquish, he didn't know how to make himself at ease with it at all.

Underneath him, Martin gave a bitten off gasp as Robin shifted, changing the way his weight was distributed and the angle of where he was impaled on Martin. Their bodies were starting to learn how to respond to one another; each of Robin's movements was matched by Martin, an up for every down.

That was its own kind of overwhelming; Robin had always thought of the shared pleasure of sex as simply being each party bringing the other to orgasm within a short window of time—one gets off and then the other gets off; everybody's happy. But sex with Martin was already beginning to feel like something else completely.

It was the two of them together, in something almost like a feedback loop of intensity. Robin's pleasure was heightened because of how good he was obviously making Martin feel. It wasn't anything like anything Robin had experienced before. Perhaps it was because he'd never cared about anyone he'd had sex with, not nearly so much as he cared about Martin.

It was the first time he'd worked to make sure his partner was feeling as good as he was, and Robin was very surprised to discover how satisfying that work was. When he raised himself up and then down again with particular vigor, his body tightening around Martin's length at the same time, it ripped a deep and uncontrolled moan from Martin's mouth. Robin folded himself down close enough to press their lips together, swallowing that sound as it spilled out of Martin. He had done that; he had wrung that pleasure out of his lover.

Martin's lips were red and swollen, and Robin wished he could scratch the smallest cut into that perfect, punished flesh. A spike of lust made his own mouth fall open at the thought of tasting Martin's blood. The intensity of the desire made him redouble his efforts to make Martin's pleasure hit the same kind of heights that Robin was experiencing.

The angle was perfect inside Robin's body, and he threw his head back, his soundless cry directed at the ceiling, his hands scrabbling against Martin's chest.

Martin's expression was beautiful, desperate. He stared up at Robin, hips thrusting up at an uneven, fast pace, too far gone to keep any kind of rhythm.

"Are you close?" Robin asked, getting a wild nod from Martin as a reply. Robin rocked down again, hard, making himself gasp.

"Yeah, yeah, let's just—hold on," Martin managed to choke out, separating their bodies for long enough to turn them so Robin's back lay against the sheets, and then pushing back into Robin with a grunt that made Robin let out a string of curses and cling to Martin's shoulders hard enough to bruise.

Martin bit at his own lip as he tried to hold back his orgasm, the level of pressure strong enough to break the thin skin with his front teeth. The smell of blood slammed against Robin's senses, his vision going white and his whole body shuddering as he came. He could feel Martin inside him, the hot pulse that told him they had reached climax almost simultaneously.

It took them a long time to come down from it, panting together in mingled breaths, Robin inhaling the lingering whisper of Martin's blood scent as the tiny tear stopped bleeding. Martin's eyes were alight, reflecting how happy and overwhelmed he was as he stared at Robin's face.

Martin might have wanted to stay midcoitus forever, fucking for eternity, but secretly this was the moment that Robin wished could be timeless. Lying together, staring at one another, marveling that someone who fitted against all his empty edges could ever exist in the world.

Years earlier, in England, Robin had seen a production of *Sleeping Beauty* choreographed by the famous Matthew Bourne. In the production, Sleeping Beauty and her true love had actually known one another before that fateful prick of blood on her finger from a spindle.

Realizing that he would be long dead before her cursed hundred years of sleeping were up, the young man in the ballet had sought out a vampire, and then he had asked to be made immortal. It was the only way he could cheat fate and exist in the same time and place as his Sleeping Beauty ever again.

When he'd seen the ballet, Robin had thought it was a mildly original, visually stunning adaptation of a classic story. Now, it seemed profound and lovely. The only thing that had ever come close, in his own hundred years of darkness, to making the long endurance of it all seem worthwhile...was this.

If he'd had some fairy story vision, back in his living life, that had told him Martin would exist a century onward from where he was...well, perhaps Robin would have made the same choice that the true love in the ballet had. Maybe he would have given up his living life and become this monster, solely for the hope that they might exist in the same time and place together someday.

Robin wondered if that was what being in love was meant to feel like. If he was even capable of love.

"We really need to clean off," Martin said quietly. "We're pretty gross right now."

"You really know how to ruin a moment," Robin retorted.

"I think it's the rapidly drying bodily fluids doing that. Come on, shower time."

The shower wasn't a particularly large one, but it was more than enough room for two people who didn't mind sharing personal space with one another. The water was hot, steam fogging the glass door and making the air around them feel lush and humid.

Robin let the stream cascade down over him, closing his eyes and letting the sensation of the water fill his mind. Martin started to clean him with small, gentle circles of the washcloth. Then he made a noise of surprise, resting his hand on Robin's chest.

"The water...your skin's absorbing the heat. You feel as warm as I am."

Robin felt a shock of panic, filled with the sudden terror that Martin liked him better like this: with the illusion that he was alive. Then the panic turned to a heavy, cold weight in Robin's stomach as he reminded himself that there was no reason to worry—of course Martin would prefer a living lover, would welcome any momentary lie that made it seem real. It was stupid for him to think otherwise, even for a moment.

Beyond that first idle remark, Martin didn't comment further on the temperature of Robin's body. Instead, he washed Robin's hair with shampoo that smelled like apples, working it in with gentle care. The tenderness made Robin feel an echo of the pleasure that Martin had given him the night before, so he remained still and let Martin do it.

Maybe he wanted the lie as much as Martin did: a brief fantasy that Robin was someone worth being looked after, something that deserved kindness.

He couldn't easily leave the house until night fell, so Robin curled up on the bed and slept, trying to shake the weight that pulled down his spirit. Martin's bed smelled like them both, like the sex they'd had there, which was distracting and comforting simultaneously.

☆☆☆

When evening fell, and Robin could venture out again without risking major burns, he made his way home. His feet felt heavy, but he knew there was no physical reason for them to do so—it took an enormous amount of lost energy before Robin would begin to actually feel weariness.

He knew it was only a matter of time before Martin realized the truth about him. Martin was such a naturally giving, generous person that it genuinely didn't occur to him that anyone might be the fundamental opposite of this: selfish, greedy, predatory. Martin made Robin want to be better, but that was impossible. Robin was a vampire. His very design was all the worst things a person was capable of.

Robin was very tired.

His home, if it deserved the term, was a small, unremarkable apartment on the third floor of a 1960s-built walk-up. It had been quite a comfortable, nicely appointed place when he'd first moved in, but in the intervening years disrepair had slowly crept over everything, and now it resembled nothing so much as a low-budget stage for a story set after the apocalypse.

None of the apartment's infrastructure was newer than the 1970s, because that's when Robin had moved in and he'd never had any impetus to keep it maintained or repaired. This was also the reason why the entire kitchen was blanketed in thick drifts of gray, gritty dust. White, half-melted candles, their holders everything from sterling silver candlesticks to repurposed glass bottles that Robin had borrowed from his neighbors' recycling, rested in whatever area of the room Robin had needed light on a given occasion. The electric lights had stopped working years ago, but the candles were enough. Robin had good eyes.

He'd never opened the oven. He suspected it would look like the rest of the kitchen, with its dry, ashy grime. But for all he knew it might be infiltrated by mice, or sealed off from the ravages of time completely. He didn't care which option was the truth of the matter; he had no need to cook food for himself, and nobody else had been inside the apartment since he moved in.

The bedroom had thick, good-quality blackout curtains that kept out every possible speck of light, because at the time when he'd had them put in, Robin had cared enough to bother. These days, he'd probably just sleep on the floor of the deep hanging closet installed along one wall. He couldn't remember why he'd even cared about giving himself a whole bedroom to be safe in during the day. Sunburn wouldn't even kill him; it would just hurt. Robin could handle pain when he needed to. It didn't matter.

His mattress had a dry, beach-sized towel draped over it, because he'd worn through the fabric covering the pillow top by not bothering with sheets for so long. There was thin foam and then wire springs, exposed up to the air as if rats had chewed through to make a nest. They hadn't; there was nothing in the apartment for them to eat, so they'd never bothered to take up residency. The ugly decrepitude of the bed had all been caused by

Robin's apathy, by the times when he'd lie there unmoving for days, sometimes weeks. But he didn't care about the exposed innards of the mattress. Once he was lying down, he found a way to be comfortable enough, and he didn't care all that much about comfort anyway.

There were stacks of books against the walls or in corners or shoved back into shelves in horizontal stacks. Sometimes Robin would contemplate how, some other day, he'd put them all back into the shelves properly, but it never felt important enough to bother with on the occasions when he remembered that it needed to be done. The procrastination had been going on for decades by now, which would have been almost impressive if he'd thought much about it. He didn't, though. It didn't really matter.

Robin owned the apartment, which was good, because he could imagine how easy it would be to lose sense of time completely. He'd only have to do that once or twice before he'd wind up evicted for unpaid rent. Or he could ask his bank to take care of it, probably, but Robin hated dealing with his bank. They always expected him to care about his money.

He had a television, a cathode-ray one of a fairly impressive size that had been close to cutting-edge when he'd bought it. These days, though, it couldn't even receive the type of signal that channels were broadcast on. Not that this mattered much; Robin only used it for playing DVDs. He'd buy five seasons of a crime drama at once and then lie on his musty sofa, watching episode after episode play on the screen.

His favorite shows were the ones it was impossible to get too invested in; the sort designed to be vaguely entertaining without really capturing the heart. They would wash over him like lukewarm waves, demanding very little from him as they played out their easily guessed stories.

He loaded one into the player now, the familiar rhythms of the predictable procedural lulling him into a numb calmness, away from the worst of his ugly thoughts.

Despite having slept for most of the day, Robin was all too happy to curl up on the couch and lie, unmoving, as the hours passed.

Chapter Six

Martin

Polly was Nora's favorite. Which, considering Nora's personality, mostly meant that Polly tolerated more from her than most other people were willing to put up with, such as near-endless repetitions of fetch and near-constant pats and attention.

The pair were currently playing a game on Martin's sofa, which involved Polly hiding a ball behind the cushions and then Nora's absolute befuddlement as to where it had gone.

"I think she thinks it respawns behind my back each time!" Polly shrieked in delight as the little dog clambered all over her, trying to look at the space behind where she was sitting. "She looks there every time, even when she's just seen me hide it behind the cushions!"

"Respawns?" Martin asked, not recognizing the term.

"Like in games," Polly explained, looking at him as if he was an uneducated buffoon. By her standards, he kind of was, Martin realized. "When you die and then show up on the map again, you do it at a respawn point, get it? Nora thinks the ball's respawn point is behind my back, and that it appears there whenever I make it disappear, no matter where it might have been just before it vanished."

Martin gave a sage nod. "Ah, I see. I get it. I think?"

Polly sighed. "You're hopeless. Go talk to Mom about boring adult stuff, and leave me and Nora alone."

"Are you throwing me out of my own living room?"

"Seems like it, yeah."

Sarah was sitting in one of the pair of patio chairs that Martin kept out the back, overlooking his small garden. She tapped the ash off the end of her cigarette into the can that served as an ashtray and gave him a tired smile. "Polly and Nora kicked you out?"

Martin nodded. "I was callously evicted."

She gestured for him to sit in the second chair, beside her. "Thanks for having us over. She loves playing with Nora."

"It's my pleasure. You know I always love seeing you guys."

"I'm pretty sure," Sarah teased in her driest tone. "That most people would agree with me that it's considered a little weird for your closest friend to be someone you issue a paycheck to every fortnight."

"If you don't want the paychecks anymore, you should have said. My accountant will be thrilled," Martin replied without missing a beat. He wasn't nearly as skilled at looking or sounding deadpan as Sarah, but he did his best with what he had.

"All I mean is, it might be good for you to have more of a life outside The Warm Taste..." Sarah trailed off, stalling the end of her sentence with another drag from her cigarette.

Martin was puzzled. "What do you mean?"

"Look, I'm hardly a saint. We both know that," Sarah said with a sigh. "I'm not going to begrudge you your early-middle-age crisis and the attendant twink boyfriend on your arm, a twink boyfriend you found in your own coffee shop..."

Martin made a face at the term and then buried the expression in his hands in dread. "Oh my god, that's what Robin is, isn't he? He's all pretty and lithe; he's a twink. I'm officially a middle-aged—"

"I said early middle-aged, Mart."

"—a middle-aged," Martin repeated, emphasizing the abject horror of the words, "man of means with a twink lover. I am the cliché."

"You're hardly Calvin Klein, dating a porn star fifty years younger than you," Sarah replied, voice still dry as dust. "All I'm saying is do whatever makes you happy. It's your life. Date a customer if you want. But be careful, okay? I get...I dunno...a vibe from him. I don't want to see you caught up in weird shit. I don't want to see you hurt."

Martin was glad his face was still covered by his palms, because he couldn't stop the momentary grin that Sarah's words caused. He couldn't begin to imagine how much more overprotective she'd be if she knew how potentially dangerous Robin really was.

Smoothing away the smile, he looked up at her. "I appreciate that. Honestly, I do. But don't worry about me. I can look after myself."

"Can you, though? You keep that dog even though she's awful, and I've never seen you fire anybody—"

"Nobody I've hired has needed firing. And Nora can't be as bad as you say if Polly loves her, right?"

"Oh, please, that child has an infinite capacity to love garbage," Sarah retorted. "You should hear the shit she puts on the speakers when we're driving anywhere."

Polly came out the back door with Nora on her heels, as if the two of them had been summoned by the discussion. She was holding a handful of movie cases, and looking extremely unimpressed.

"All your Disney movies are old and dumb and you don't have any Pixar."

"Excuse me." Martin raised his eyebrows. "*Lilo and Stitch* is not old."

She turned the DVD case over and checked the technical credits. "This says it was made in 2002."

"Two thousand and two is not..." Martin's shoulders slumped. "Shit, I am so old. That is so depressing."

Polly giggled.

"The movie's good, though. It's way better than Pixar," Martin insisted, unable to stop himself from making a face along with the final word.

"*You don't like Pixar?*" Polly's eyes went wide. "You're an inhuman monster."

No, just dating one, Martin thought in amusement. Aloud, he said, "I just don't think they have very good messages. Like how *Toy Story* has a bad guy who's just this weird poor kid who likes to be creative with his toys. It's not like he has any reason to suspect he lives in a universe where they're more than just lumps of plastic. I think it's pretty classist and screwed up. And *Wall-E* treats a pair of robots as more deserving of our empathy than fat people. And *The Incredibles* is just blatant objectivist propaganda—"

Sarah, standing up, patted her daughter on the shoulder. "Sorry, kiddo. Martin turns into a crazy person when people bring up Pixar."

"They all convey the message that if you're not fulfilling a useful purpose, you're without worth," Martin insisted. "It's messed up!"

"Ugh, you are so weird." Polly made a face at him. "You are the weirdest. You don't like Pixar, and all your anime is old and dumb and full of robots." Her tone made it clear that these were some of the most cutting observations ever made by one human being about another. "I have to teach you everything. I'm going to bring over some good movies next time."

The three of them ate dinner together; a risotto that Martin made followed by vanilla ice cream Sarah had brought with her. They'd discovered over the years that it was easier to get Polly to eat if the food she was being offered was pale—mashed potatoes, white bread, plain pasta. Since it was important to get as many calories into Polly as they could manage, Martin and Sarah had learned to eat the bland fare with aplomb, if not always genuine enjoyment.

Now that she was old enough to venture into slightly more complex rice dishes, the ordeal had become a little easier. The meal had taste to it, at least.

Martin found himself wondering if Robin's experience of drinking blood to survive ever echoed this same feeling; of eating simply in order to have eaten. Obviously there was a pleasurable dimension to the act, for Robin and his victim both, but aside from that intimacy...was blood tasty? Was it delicious? Or was it a diet restriction so strict that it almost became a chore—nothing but mashed potatoes, night after night for all eternity.

After dinner they took Nora for a walk, with Polly correcting all the ways in which Martin was doing it wrong and eventually just taking Nora's lead for herself. He could already see how infuriating she was destined to become as her teen years went on, and how frayed Sarah's patience was already growing with the know-it-all attitude, but Martin continued to find it endearing.

Martin couldn't imagine his life without Polly and Sarah. They'd made him believe in family again after his parents had broken the part of him that trusted and loved; they'd knit the ruined threads of caring that were left of him back into something that was brave enough to care about people again.

He held out for an entire thirty-five minutes after saying goodnight to them as they left before he texted Robin, which was a length of time Martin felt more proud of than he should have. Although, he surmised, feeling absurd over feeling proud about it probably canceled out any genuine pride, really.

The point was the thought of Robin turned Martin into some kind of reckless, hedonistic teenager, one who couldn't even manage to take his date out somewhere civilized for a proper, reasonable outing. Instead, all he wanted to do was be alone with Robin, touch Robin, fall into bed with Robin as soon as an opportunity presented itself.

He confessed all that to Robin, when Robin showed up at his house. Well, not immediately after Robin showed up at his house. First, they kissed in the doorway for a while. Then they kissed on the sofa for an even longer while. Then Martin confessed just how ridiculous Robin made him feel.

"I wondered for a little while if there was some aphrodisiac thing going on," he told Robin. "That maybe vampires had a pheromone they gave off to make people let them into their personal space more intimately. But you seem to be able to go about your life without everyone throwing themselves at you all the time. Everyone but me, anyway."

Robin chuckled. "I don't have anything like that. Not that I know of, at any rate. For a while I wondered the same about you, actually. If there was something about you because of your scent, and…"

An expression that almost looked like guilt crossed his face. Then Robin shook off the momentary strangeness and kissed Martin.

"I think the real answer is that we just happen to have excellent chemistry."

"Mmm. Good answer."

They stayed like that for a long time, just lazily making out on the sofa. One of Robin's hands made its way up underneath Martin's shirt to rest against his chest. He stroked a nipple in lazy circles. Robin wound up lying on top of Martin, his soft hair under

Martin's palm and between Martin's fingers, the toothpaste taste of his mouth against Martin's own.

Their tryst was abruptly interrupted by Nora, who jumped first onto the sofa and then onto Robin's back, demanding their attention with a series of sharp barks.

It ruined the moment completely. Robin buried his laughter against Martin's shoulder and then climbed off the sofa, collecting Nora in his arms along the way.

"Sounds like someone was sick of being ignored," he noted, grinning.

"She's already been out for a trip around the block this evening," Martin said as he stood up as well. "But let's take her out for a longer walk anyway. Hopefully that should tire her out enough that she'll leave us alone for a while, once we get back."

In the end, they decided to risk taking Nora to the college campus, despite the likelihood of her barking at innocent students for absolutely no reason. She was sometimes skittish about going for twilight adventures, but seemed happy enough to inspect this new and exciting location, pulling on her leash excitedly in an endless but futile effort to get her human to walk faster.

There was a wide lawn of grass with benches near it, so Martin let Nora go free and the pair of them claimed one of the seats, watching her run around happily as she reveled in the open space and fresh evening air.

As they sat on the bench, Martin was struck by how well Robin fit into his surroundings. It was more than the natural ability to blend into the background that Robin had, and it wasn't just the fact that his apparent age was the same as that of the majority of the students going about their lives around the pair of them.

It was the mix of world-weariness and curiosity that Robin had about everything, the competing desires to retreat from and engage with the busy flow of life all around. Martin had seen a lot of students come into The Warm Taste to study, over the years, and he recognized that mix as something they'd all had, to a greater or lesser degree.

Martin couldn't help but wonder if Robin truly had that air about him from being so old, as Martin had first assumed, or if it was rather caused by the fact that Robin had died so young.

Either way, maybe Robin would feel more connected to the world if he realized there were places where people like him felt right at home.

"Have you ever thought about going to night school?"

Robin didn't answer immediately. After a minute of quiet, his eyes narrowed in thought, he finally replied. "Even the thought of it is exhausting. I'm tired just contemplating whether I'd enjoy it or not."

"It wouldn't be that bad," Martin objected.

"Yes, it would. It wouldn't just be a matter of studying whatever subject I decided on. First of all I'd have to study the people doing that type of course, so I could learn how to blend in. How to look normal. Do you have any idea how exhausting that is?"

Robin's question was rhetorical, but Martin answered it anyway. "Yeah, I do, actually. Vampires aren't the only ones who have to fake that they fit in with everyone else, you know."

Robin looked abashed. "Sorry. I didn't mean it like that. I just meant that it'd be a lot of work, and I don't really see much reason to bother."

Martin accepted the answer with a nod, and the two of them sat in companionable silence for a while as Nora performed her important detective work of smelling patches of grass and the base of every tree she could find.

"You had Sarah and Polly over today?" Robin asked, breaking the quiet.

"Yeah, how'd you know?"

"I could smell Sarah's cigarettes when I came over. Also, every cartoon DVD you own was stacked up on the table."

Martin laughed. "Polly's decided I have bad taste in movies."

"They mean a lot to you, don't they? Polly and Sarah."

Martin could feel his own expression soften, his smile small and sincere as he nodded. "Yeah. They do. I've known them since Polly was really small. Sarah was pretty young when she had her, and man, she loves that kid with her whole heart and soul."

He thought back to the first time he'd encountered his spiky, generous best friend. "When I met them, it was because Sarah was going around to all the local coffee shops and asking if they'd consider having a special change jar on the counter, so customers could give a few bucks toward Polly's medical bills if they wanted to."

Robin's mouth quirked, for a moment, into a slight smile. "And you put as much in as she would let you, didn't you?"

"You know it," Martin admitted. "And I gave her a job. She'd lost her last one because of all the hours she had to be with Polly. I admired her so much. No matter how bad things got, Sarah never let herself give up. She slept in hospital chairs and then turned up to work a full shift—which, of course, I'd try to refuse to let her do, promising I'd pay her for her time while she went home to sleep. The only reason I always gave in and wound up letting her do the work is because she said it was easier to cope with the heartache if she had something to distract her."

He stretched his arms, the weight of history and hard memories making his muscles feel tense. "We've always done all right. At The Warm Taste, I mean. The business grew faster than I really knew how to cope with, so a lot of it turned into a trial by fire. It's kind of amazing it stayed running through a lot of it, looking back on everything, honestly. But now, aside from occasional bad days—like recently, when the power was out practically all morning; that was a disaster—aside from those days, I think I'm mostly on top of it now. I know what I'm doing. It's a pretty cool feeling. Unlike most of my generation, it turns out I kind of like being an adult."

Nora came back to where they sat, jumping up onto the bench between them and climbing onto Martin's lap with her usual air of absolute entitlement.

"And then there's this little miss. I'd always wanted to get a pet again; I had a cat when I was a kid and I'd adored her. But as an adult I always kept putting it off. I figured I should wait until I had everything settled, you know? I wasn't sure what kind of sign from the heavens above or whatever would show up to tell me that I was ready, but I felt like it'd be obvious, you know?"

Robin laughed. "If you still think like that, you aren't an adult yet, you're just old."

"Yeah, yeah, shut up," Martin shot back, grinning. "I know that now. I kind of worked it out when I ended up buying a dog as an impulse purchase when I was out shopping for groceries. I know it's awful and shitty to get dogs from a pet store rather than from a shelter, but she was there in the window, the last dog left, sitting there alone in the glass display without anything to entertain her—no friends, no toys, just a little dish of food in the corner and shredded newspaper to sleep on. She was a tiny, tiny thing; I felt sure she must've been taken away from her mother at an earlier age than puppies are ready for that. She just looked miserable, and all at once all the thoughts about shelters and about waiting until the universe showed me that I was ready...none of that mattered, as I looked at that forlorn little creature, staring out at the passersby. So I bought her and took her home."

"Little did you know you'd bought a monster?"

Martin laughed. "Yeah. Of course, it didn't take long before her personality started showing. She chewed on everything. I mean everything. Polly used to have a tub of art supplies here, but we decided it was better if Sarah took it back to her place after Nora ate a tube of silver glitter while I had my back turned. Do you have any idea how weird dog shit looks when it's got silver glitter all through it? Because I do, from personal experience. She chewed on my pillows until they spilled open. She refused to be house trained—at first I thought it was just that she'd been taken from her mother so early that she didn't understand how to learn skills like that, but then after a while I realized that no, it wasn't that at all. She understood well enough about crapping outside. She just didn't care. Even now, when it's raining or especially cold outside, she just does it indoors. She's a rotten little sociopath."

"You seem to have a propensity for those. I'm not judging or anything," Robin said, absolutely deadpan. "I'm just saying. Your dog's some kind of reincarnated criminal, and you're dating a bloodthirsty creature of the night."

"Well, since you're the aforementioned bloodthirsty creature of the night, you've gotta at least respect her right to be who she is. At the time, everyone told me I should try to find someone to take her off my hands. It suddenly seemed like everyone had some friend-of-a-friend who absolutely loved little dogs just like her, even when they were wretched little monsters. Nobody could understand why I'd keep her when it was obvious we were the worst possible fit for each other as pet and human."

Martin shrugged and gave Robin a lopsided smile. "What nobody could comprehend, and yet seemed the most obvious thing in the world to me, was that she was a wretched little monster, sure, but...she was *my* wretched little monster. Once I got her, I got her for life. I...I want to be the opposite of my parents. That's my major philosophy in everything I do: to love as unconditionally as I can, always. To never give up on anyone just because loving them isn't what I expected, or requires more work than I thought it would. I will never let myself become what my parents were. I will never give up on somebody just because the going gets tough."

Robin gave Martin a doubtful look. "That sounds like a really easy way to get hurt, or to trap yourself in situations that you'd be better off leaving. Do you have borderlines for that philosophy?"

Then Robin stopped and laughed hollowly. "What am I saying? If I tell you to learn how to ditch toxic people, I'm going to be down one boyfriend. I'm not nearly selfless enough to do that 'if you love something, set it free' kind of thinking."

"Even if you did try to break up with me for my own good, it's my decision to be here with you," Martin reminded him. "You don't get a say in what I do or don't do. I'd only leave if you truly didn't want to be with me anymore, for your own reasons. Not on my behalf. And was that—" His voice shifted from earnest to teasing. "—the word love I just heard you use?"

Robin rolled his eyes. "I changed my mind. We're breaking up."

Still in a good mood, they walked back to Martin's home and relaxed together in the living room. Lying on the sofa together, each with a book to read, was one of those small, simple pleasures that Martin felt inordinately happy to enjoy with Robin.

Dating a beautiful, tragic vampire was very romantic, obviously, but Martin wasn't quite the right kind of person to properly appreciate the dark beauty of that kind of thing. He liked his dog and coffee and reading. He was a pretty prosaic guy.

Basically, he was a terrible candidate to be dating Robin, and yet here they were. The sofa was long enough for each of them to use an arm rest as a pillow and then have their feet and ankles meet on the center cushion to intertwine.

Martin's book of choice was *The Midwich Cuckoos*, which he liked to reread every few years or so, and always got something new out of each time he revisited it. He'd always felt a deep pang of sympathy for the eerie race of children in the story—they weren't evil, just different, and everyone else was too frightened of them to try to find any sort of common ground with them. It was a tragedy, underneath its science fiction trappings.

Robin began by leafing through a book of Martin's about the library of Oscar Wilde, but soon put it off to one side and stared up at the ceiling. "I've read this one through twice already, but the thought of looking for something new is too exhausting."

"I can make an attempt to pick you something," Martin offered, the idea filling him with energy and enthusiasm. "What kind of book do you feel like? Fiction, non-fiction, old, new..."

"Not fiction," Robin replied immediately. "It's stupid, I know, but I can't bring myself to read fiction."

"That's not stupid at all. I've gone through lots of periods of my life like that," Martin assured him.

Robin looked shocked. "I had no idea that other people went through that. Are you serious?"

"Yeah, of course. Let me find you something cool, give me a minute." Martin got up from the couch and went over to one of the bookshelves. He hummed a little to himself as he considered and rejected each of the titles. After a minute, his eyes found the perfect one, and he pulled it out with a triumphant smile.

The book he handed Robin was *The Zhivago Affair: the Kremlin, the CIA, and the Battle Over a Forbidden Book.*

"It's about America's attempts to undermine Russia during the Cold War, by smuggling in banned art. Pretty cool," Martin offered. "Though if you'd like something drier, I can look."

"I'll give this one a try and let you know," Robin replied.

The two of them settled back into their positions on the sofa, with Nora joining them a short while later to lie across their intertwined ankles and hold them both captive at once.

Lulled by the slow, gentle atmosphere, Martin gave a wide yawn, which in turn made Robin yawn as well a few seconds later. Martin blinked, a wide smile slowly spreading on his face.

"Hey. You yawned."

"Did I?" Robin put the book down on his chest, holding his place open. "I guess I did, yeah. So?"

"Psychopaths don't, you know. Yawn. When someone else does, they don't automatically do it. too. That's an empathy thing. But you yawned, so the next time you're feeling shitty about yourself, remember that. You yawned. You're not a monster."

Robin gave him a smile in response; one that Martin could instantly tell meant Robin wasn't at all convinced by the claim.

"I'm a creature that thrives through invisibility," Robin said in a rueful voice. "Of course I naturally mimic the traits of the species I blend in amongst." He nodded toward the paperback in Martin's hand. "I'm like a cuckoo egg hiding in a nest."

Martin made a small scoffing sound. "That was a very awkward use of a simile."

"Probably," Robin conceded with a grin, maneuvering himself down to Martin's end of the couch by crawling up the length of Martin's body.

They made out for a while, at the same lazy pace they'd been lying together reading. Martin couldn't imagine that he'd ever want anything more than this in the whole rest of his life: just Robin, Robin's touch and Robin's mouth and, best of all, the feeling of Robin's smile against his own, the quiet sound of Robin's laugh in those moments when Martin managed to make him feel particularly happy.

Eventually, Robin pulled away a little. "Mmm, I should go home," he said, sounding regretful. "I've been putting off cleaning my place for basically forever. You'd be shocked at how much procrastination living forever can generate."

"Want me to come help? I'm pretty good with a mop."

"No, go rest. It'll be impetus for me make the apartment nice, if I know I'm missing out on lying next to you. Who knows, maybe I'll even make it nice enough that you can visit it someday. Wouldn't that be something?"

They said good-bye to one another and Robin left.

Martin, tidying up before going to bed, saw that Robin had left the book about Zhivago behind. Espionage and illegal Russian novels made for non-fiction that was too close to fiction, then. Martin picked up the book and returned it to the shelf.

He wondered how much of Robin's isolation came from assuming that nobody else had experienced quite the same dark moments as himself, like when he had been so surprised to discover that Martin, too, had gone through times in his life when fiction had asked too much of him as a reader.

Martin wanted to find ways to help Robin connect more with the world so that Robin could begin to understand he wasn't as monstrous and strange as he assumed. Maybe he could make a few friends—Martin had seen him chatting to that red-haired kid who came to the coffee shop to study once in a while. Sometimes the guy came in with small children, too; a few different ones. He'd told Sarah he was a babysitter, hadn't he? They must be his charges.

And he was good with Polly, too, from the one instance Martin had seen of them interacting. Anyone who was tolerated by Polly had to have a particularly high level of skill in dealing with children.

Martin realized he didn't actually know how Robin felt about kids. It must have been difficult for him, to see young people, people with so much potential stretching out before them, when

Robin's own potential had been interrupted so irrevocably. Robin would never grow up all the way, after all.

But Martin would do his best to make Robin's life happy and full, despite the stumbling blocks. It wasn't up to only him—he knew the ultimate choice as to whether he wanted to engage with the world was Robin's to make—but Martin could at least help it along, couldn't he?

Martin was just about to get into bed when his phone chimed with a text from Robin.

I want your cock inside me again already. You should fuck me so hard I forget my own name and all I can do is howl like a dog at how good you make me feel.

It gave Martin a swell of desire, and made him grin. But he must really be getting old, because instead of dialing Robin's number for a round of phone sex, and even instead of jerking off, Martin just put the phone back on his dresser and fell asleep.

☆☆☆

The next morning was gray and overcast; the threat of rain practically tangible in the cold air. But the rain itself hadn't begun, not yet, so Martin decided to press his luck and take Nora out for her morning walk anyway.

It paid off, but only just. They were barely back inside before a full-fledged storm began; the lightning and thunder coming one after the other at such a fast pace it seemed like the worst of it must be right overhead. Nora immediately slunk underneath the sofa, which was her go-to spot for hiding from the worst possible dangers, such as storms or fire alarms.

Martin watched the rain through a window for a while, wondering if he should wait it out and arrive at The Warm Taste slightly late, or brave the downpour and risk spending the rest of the day in damp socks. This wasn't the kind of rain that could be held off by a mere umbrella.

He decided to head out at his usual time, despite the weather. After all, it might not let up for hours yet—at this time of year, it wasn't easy to predict how things would go. Chances were that he'd end up having to walk through the rain anyway, even if he waited until he was late for work. Martin strongly disliked being late, and the payoff of hesitating was too uncertain to make it worthwhile.

In a strange way, it was actually kind of nice to walk in the chilly storm. Nobody else was foolhardy enough to be out and about, and all the colors that were usually present in the homes and stores on Martin's block were washed to shades of gray. It was like trying to walk to work through a particularly gloomy noir movie.

As expected, his umbrella was only slightly useful at best. The cuffs of his shirt and the hems of his pants, not to mention his shoes, were all uncomfortably wet by the time Martin got to The Warm Taste. He shook his umbrella out as best he could before closing it and bringing it inside, stashing it in a bucket they left by the door on days like these. There were a few others already in there, owned by patrons who were scattered around the shop, each of them sipping a warm drink and looking as mildly drenched as Martin felt.

Sarah was working the counter, talking quietly with a miserable-looking young woman who was buying a coffee. The young woman had eyes bruised from sleeplessness, the rims of them wearing the smeary blue-black traces of mascara. She thanked Sarah for the coffee and left the shop, stepping out into the downpour as if she didn't even feel the cold rain striking her worn jacket and messy hair.

"I didn't realize we were already deep into the student meltdown stage of the semester," Martin quipped as he reached where Sarah stood. She flinched at the joke, and Martin's stomach went leaden as he realized that the young woman's distress must have been real and true, about more than simple exam worries. She must have been giving Sarah bad news.

It had happened the same way often enough in the past that all Martin asked was, "Who?"

Sarah let out a long sigh, her shoulders slumping heavily. "He's alive, at least. That's the important part. It was Ben, you remember him?"

Martin sorted through his mental collection of patron names. "That friendly kid who helped Polly with her phone?"

Sarah nodded. Martin swore under his breath. "You said he was alive. Is he going to be okay?"

"He stepped out in front of a tram. He almost lost his arm," Sarah replied. "I know we don't usually do much when this sorta thing happens, but I was thinking we could maybe send flowers or something? Polly's gonna be sad if she finds out what happened. She doesn't like most people, but she liked him. I got his hospital room details off his friend."

Martin nodded. "Yeah, yeah. That sounds good. Give the details here. I'll set it all up."

Chapter Seven

Robin

In Robin's opinion, hospitals were pretty much the crappiest locations in the entire universe.

He knew objectively that hospitals had a huge number of positive purposes. They were where people healed from injury, and were treated for illnesses. It was where suffering was minimized. New lives started in hospitals every day, even if those births weren't without their own unique traumas.

Even so, Robin loathed them. He hated the scents of fevered wounds and medicines, of reheated food and harsh cleaning products that never fully hid the smells of ailing human bodies. He associated that symphony of elements on the air with a unique strain of brutality that he couldn't put a name to; he would have blamed this association on the hospital he'd been in during the war, but felt quite certain that he would have felt it regardless of his own experiences.

It was the first time in many years that he'd set foot inside a hospital, and in the decades since the last occasion a new note had joined the familiar ones in the bouquet: machinery. Robin could hardly fathom the amount of electronic equipment in the rooms and floors around him. Humans would only be able to hear and smell a fraction of what Robin could but, even so, he couldn't help but imagine that all those alarms and beeps and whirrs and all the other metallic and digital noises were grating even on dulled, living ears.

The efficiency of the nurses as they went about their work reminded Robin of Sarah. They had her same friendly professionalism; a natural kindness toward everyone they dealt with. A desire to do good work, teamed with a self-preservation that allowed emotional distance.

It was evening, well past official visiting hours, but Martin had assured Robin that it wouldn't be a problem. "Nobody stops you when you're walking down a hospital corridor with a bunch of flowers, trust me. I've visited Polly at all hours over the years and never had an issue."

"And he knows we're coming?" Robin reconfirmed. "It's not going to be a surprise visit out of the blue?"

"He knows we're coming. It's fine. Are you okay? You seem like you're freaking out."

Robin managed to give Martin a tight smile. "It's no big deal. Just not a big fan of hospitals."

The explanation was standard enough that Martin took it at face value.

Ben had his own room, small enough that Robin felt as if they were crowding it by entering. He guessed, from the moldings on the window and the proportions of the space, that it was at least eighty years old, perhaps ninety. No amount of clever designing and arranging could make the room large enough to comfortably fit all the modern equipment that needed to be around the bed, and so the overall effect was of a room with more furniture than air. There weren't any flowers visible, or "best wishes" cards left out on display.

Ben himself was lying in the bed, his arm encircled above the elbow with a metal, cage-like device with pins that went into his skin all around, and below the elbow with a cast that reached down to the knuckles of his hand. He had a hospital gown and a drip and looked extremely the worse for wear and more than a little miserable.

He also appeared incredibly surprised to see Robin and Martin. Robin shot Martin a glare. Martin radiated completely unconvincing innocence.

"How did you guys know I was here?" Ben asked, confirming Robin's suspicion that Martin was a filthy liar.

"One of your classmates came into The Warm Taste to grab some notes you'd left there accidentally," explained Martin.

"Oh, Tabitha, right. She was just meant to check for the pages; see if they were still there. I thought maybe they could help her out with some stuff we were both struggling with. I figured that they'd almost certainly been tossed out as garbage—they were just handwritten sheets. Realizing I'd lost them was kind of the..." Ben shook himself, cutting off his own words with a smile that was as completely unconvincing as Martin's had been. "Anyway, she wasn't supposed to tell everyone that I was here, in the hospital. I had no idea she would."

"Well, she did, and here we are," Martin told him.

"But...why?" Ben carried deep confusion in his voice and expression.

"You're good with Polly," Martin answered, as if the answer was simple and obvious. "Most people aren't."

"That still doesn't seem like a sufficient reason," insisted Ben, looking even more puzzled. "Like, at all."

Martin appeared to ignore the objection, glancing around the room. Robin had already assessed the space as they entered; his natural hunter's instincts taking in details that humans had to make an effort to consciously notice. Martin, like Robin, would be noticing there were no flowers or cards on the nightstand or windowsill, and no scent of any earlier visitors remaining.

"Do you have any family that needs to be notified that you're here? I could give them a call for you." Martin's voice was carefully nonchalant. Understanding swept suddenly over Ben's face; Robin watched as the young man realized that Martin and Robin were there, at least in part, to check that someone was looking out for Ben.

Ben's reply was as much a study in deliberately casual tones as Martin's question had been. "Nah. I'm legally emancipated, so even if I was underage I wouldn't be obligated to give their info to the hospital. Things will just be easier if they don't know."

Martin gave a quiet hum of understanding.

Robin had seen a lot of people actively chase death, over the years. There was something in them that reacted when they came close enough to him, something that would draw them even closer. It made him angry and sad to think that the momentary friendly connection he'd felt with Ben had just been motivated by Ben's unconscious sense that Robin had the ability to murder with ease and efficiency.

Robin had seen a lot of those death-chasers survive, as well, and he knew very well the guilt and relief on their faces whenever they failed to die. When the jump wasn't quite high enough to be a certainty, or the pills came up as easily as they went down, or the rope broke. Robin envied that guilty, relieved look more than any other. Those people had put one foot over the threshold into the dark place where Robin dwelt, and then they had the chance to step back from it.

"Why?" Robin blurted out, feeling angry and upset.

The question didn't seem to confuse Ben even for a moment. He clearly knew exactly what Robin meant.

"It was just...things. Do I really have to explain it?"

"No," Robin answered. "I get it. But yes, I...I just don't even know what I'm trying to say." He felt concerned and angry, and he didn't understand why he felt that way. He didn't understand anything.

"Everyone thinks it was an accident. Everyone—until you—just assumed because I've tried to be upbeat about it."

The noise Robin made was one of someone who is deeply unimpressed. "Because that's totally normal, being chipper after your arm and shoulder get fucked up by a tram, and you nearly get killed by it."

Ben offered a wan smile. "Yeah. Christ, I feel so fucking guilty now. At the time I...I couldn't really think about anything but making everything that was going around and around in my head just stop. That was the only thing that I had room in my brain to care about. But now that...I guess now that the moment is passed, or maybe now that I'm on all these painkillers for my arm, so I'm kind of numb and high all at once...now that it's different, I have room in my brain to imagine how much it must have fucked up all the people who were riding on the tram when it happened. I should have done it a different way. Maybe I shouldn't have done it at all."

"There's no maybe," Robin said, his voice coming out more sharply than he had intended it to. "You're so young; you have no idea how vast the world is, how many different paths a life can travel down if you choose them. If you hate being Ben, then fuck it, fine. Throw up your hands and walk away from being him. But to give up entirely is a terrible insult to those who never had the option to keep going."

Ben blinked in surprise, obviously taken aback by the vicious passion that Robin's words had gained by the end. "I...you're right. I'm sorry."

"Don't be sorry. Be resolute. You have the opportunity to make amends for all the people you've bruised with this—your friend from class, the people on the tram, the hospital staff who have to look after you. You owe the human race a debt now, but luckily you have a second chance to do things right." Robin gave Ben a crooked smile. "Those don't come along that often, trust me."

Their conversation was interrupted by a knock at the door from an orderly. She came into the room with a tray in her hands. The evening meal that was brought in for Ben was a bowl of potato and leek soup with a bread roll and butter on the side.

"It's actually pretty tasty," Ben told them. "Way better than I expected."

"You've got a student's palate, though," Martin argued. "I've seen the stuff you kids are willing to eat. Dry noodle cakes. Beans straight from the can. Cereal with beer. I know better than to trust the word of anyone in your age and position to have acceptable standards as to what constitutes a meal."

Ben smiled. "This much is probably true. But it's also true that hospital food has a really notorious reputation, right?"

"Sure. It's bland and gross, everyone knows that."

"Well, even if your opinion on my taste isn't that high, the food here is better than the traditional view on what hospital food is supposed to be like. Look, I even got a brownie for dessert! Pretty special."

"If you say so," Martin replied, sounding dubious.

"The coffee is flat-out terrible, though. They give you a waxed cup full of hot water and a little packet of instant crystals, and you gotta just stir them in yourself. No milk or sweetener or anything; just a futile struggle to get the coffee to dissolve into the water by moving it around with a plastic spoon. And the spoon goes soft and bendy after it's in the hot water for a while. That can't be healthy, right?"

"I promise you a proper, bells-and-whistles coffee, free of charge the next time you visit The Warm Taste," Martin assured Ben.

"How do you make any money whatsoever, if you give away

coffees so often?" retorted Ben.

"I'll find a way to get you to pay me back for it."

"Yeah, that would be good. I could help out or something. I used to do busboy work when I was in high school, back home. I'm sure I haven't forgotten the trick of washing pots out, or cleaning tables."

"Give me a call when you're out of here, and we'll set up a meeting, then," Martin said. Ben nodded.

"Sure, thanks." The words were cut off from one another by an enormous yawn.

"We should leave you to sleep," decided Robin. Wasn't being tired bad for healing? Would their being here for a visit mean that Ben's recovery would be slower now? Robin hated how easy it was for the human body to become frail and begin failing. He hated the vulnerability each and every person had.

"Thanks for coming to say hi," Ben said, setting the half-eaten dinner aside and lying down as best he could. "I'll see you when I'm out of here."

"Sure thing. Get well soon, okay?"

"Oh, hey," Ben called as Robin and Martin headed toward the door. "Elisa Sánchez Loriga and Marcela Gracia Ibeas. Those were the names of those two Spanish ladies who got married that you told me about, the ones you said I should do my presentation on."

The words made Robin feel even more exhausted than he had moments earlier. Real names, with family names included no less, made the women real, too. It made them more than a story; it made them real people who had loved each other and who had suffered deeply as a result of that love. He was so tired.

They rode the elevator down to the ground floor in silence, Martin glancing over at Robin with a concerned expression. Robin didn't bother to explain.

As they walked away from the hospital together, Martin spoke quietly.

"I don't know if this will be any kind of comfort or consolation. But I've seen all of this stuff happen before. Sometimes kids get buried under the weight of what they're going through."

"He didn't seem like it," Robin managed to answer. "He seemed fine."

"Most of them do, until you've got hindsight to work with." Martin sighed, and put his arm around Robin's shoulder comfortingly. Robin leaned into the touch, grateful beneath the blankness he felt.

"I'm just glad it didn't work," Martin went on. "Sometimes I'll hear later about a kid who died, someone who was a regular, and it'll be someone I never even imagined could've been in danger of that. But it's too late by then; they're gone. The ones that it can happen to are as invisible as you are, blending in."

Robin felt strange. Not numb, exactly—he knew what numbness felt like. This was a different sort of distance; a disconnect from the world around him, like when an audio track on a movie was half a frame out of sync with the visuals.

He shook his head, trying to clear it. It didn't quite work, but when Martin began speaking again, Robin found he could largely ignore the feeling.

"I'm planning to go home and hug my dog and watch episodes of *Parks and Rec* all night if you want to join in."

Robin considered confessing that he'd never seen the show but decided that particular revelation was probably best left until for an occasion when Martin would have the emotional energy to be properly enthusiastic about making Robin watch as much as possible. It seemed wrong to waste that moment on an evening when neither of them would really have their hearts in it.

"I've got stuff I should do," Robin answered, giving Martin a quick kiss good-bye. "I'll see you later."

☆☆☆

They'd gone to the hospital almost immediately after sundown, so The Warm Taste was still open by the time Robin arrived there. He'd gone for a long, roundabout walk beforehand, trying to clear his head of the dark mess of thoughts seething inside it, but it hadn't been making him feel any better no matter what, so eventually he'd given up. Maybe being somewhere familiar would help, instead.

Ben's absence shouldn't have made all that much of a difference. He wasn't there every night, or anything like that. Under ordinary circumstances Robin may not have even noticed he wasn't there, and if he had noticed it would have been an idle thought at most.

Knowing where Ben really was, though, made the whole thing completely different. Now it was glaringly obvious to Robin that he wasn't there.

It hurt.

The hurt confused Robin. Why did something like that matter? How could he have become entangled so quickly; and why did having a greater number of people in the sphere of his life make him feel lonelier than ever?

Sarah was behind the counter and seemed pleased to see him. Robin ordered a coffee, hardly paying attention to which specifics he asked for. He'd be throwing it out without tasting it anyway, so it wasn't as if the taste mattered.

He sat down. The people around him in the coffee shop—the students and the shoppers and the couples and the readers and the ones on their phones and the ones who were working—every single one of them looked so organic, so fleshy and impermanent and vulnerable.

Robin was almost tempted to ask if Sarah needed any help, just to distract himself. He couldn't do the more complex tasks involved in preparing the orders, but she could probably teach him how to ring up prices on the cash register in a relatively short amount of time, and he could clean up tables after they had been vacated, and...

And what kind of stupid fantasy was this? He wasn't some lost young man in need of connection and friendship, like Ben was. Any sadness that Robin felt was well deserved. He was a monster. He'd never be truly connected to the world.

He left the coffee shop, not bothering to say good-bye to Sarah before doing so. It was still early enough in the evening that there were a fair number of pedestrians on the sidewalk, an even split between day people on their way home and night people on their way out. Robin chose a likely-looking group of the second sort and began to follow them.

They wound up at a small, dark bar, the kind that spent a lot of money to look as authentic and unplanned as possible. All the chairs and stools were mismatched, and the walls were hung with artfully faded vintage posters. Robin looked around at the people who were already there. Most of them were still on their first or second drink, nowhere near inebriation this soon into their night's plans.

There were a few who were considerably further along in their drinking, though. Robin's gaze lingered on one in particular: he was closer to Robin's apparent age than he was to Martin's, but he had dark hair and dark eyes like Martin, and though he was sitting down, Robin was willing to guess that he was quite tall.

With the sharp eye of a predator, Robin appraised the man and then approached, putting on a bright smile as he did so.

☆☆☆

Two hours later, he stood on Martin's doorstep and rapped his knuckles against the door, listening as Nora barked happily at the sounds of a visitor's arrival.

Martin was dressed in a very threadbare Simpsons T-shirt and a pair of sweatpants. It didn't look like he'd been asleep. When he saw Robin, his first expression was happy surprise, but a half second later it shifted to wariness.

Robin hadn't looked at his reflection on the way, so he had no idea what he looked like, but judging from Martin's reaction, the answer probably wasn't all that positive.

He made his voice falsely bright and cheerful. "I met a drunk student! It's a long time since I've had alcohol. I never really bothered. Or maybe I held off because it was dangerous. But now I can't remember why I bothered holding off since it's not like it matters. Nothing matters."

Martin opened the door wider. "Come inside before you fall over."

Robin did. The room swayed slightly around him.

"He fell over when I was finished. But..." Robin laughed. "He drank a lot before I drank a lot, so he might have fallen over even if I hadn't been there. And he was home already. As far as he's going to remember, he just had too many on his night out and then passed out on his living room floor. Not that much harm done. Not...not that it matters."

He was feeling a little sick but decided to stay standing.

Martin stayed standing, too. Robin didn't look at him. Robin didn't want to see what his expression was.

"You picked up someone who was drunk, fed from him, and then took away their memory of what happened?"

Robin couldn't see what Martin's face looked like, but the tone of his voice sounded like he was filled with disgust. Good. It was about time Martin faced the truth of what Robin was really like.

"You sound angry. Are you jealous?" Robin teased, a nasty smile curling on his lips. He looked at Martin. Martin's face was pale, his mouth a thin line.

"You're drunk." Martin pinched the bridge of his nose. "Sleep it off, and we'll talk about it later."

"You should care more, you know. You should be angrier. You should think I'm a monster for doing that to someone," Robin told him, determined to press the issue.

"Choose an angle, Robin! Do you want me to listen to moral lessons from you, or be outraged at your own lack of morals? Why are you determined to find a way to make me angry with you tonight?"

Robin shrugged, feeling churlish. "Maybe. Maybe you're not capable of understanding the reasons why I do things. We aren't even the same life form, remember."

"Go home and sleep it off. If you're still gunning for an argument tomorrow, we can hash this out then. But for now, go home." Martin's voice was cold.

Robin thought of his apartment, and how hard he'd worked to begin the task of scrubbing it back to something livable after year upon year of neglect. It made him laugh at himself, laugh and laugh and laugh, the bitterness like bile in his mouth.

"What's the point of bothering to shelve books and sweep floors? Why do people go to night school? Why do they try?" he asked Martin, voice thin and high from the stupid, stupid hilarity of it all. "What's the point of caring about people? Making friends? Everyone's so...so fragile, and they die, and it's so, so much worse than if you never cared in the first place! What's the fucking point?"

Martin's expression shifted abruptly, as if he suddenly understood what was going on, as if everything had fallen into place. "Ben didn't die, Robin."

"But he will! Everyone will. And I'll be left to remember and mourn, and I'll have to choose all over again between not caring about anything and how terrible that feels, or the horror of letting myself give a damn about the impermanent and then being left behind when time passes, and you age and you die." Robin's breaths were heaving, ragged, his throat raw and aching on every inhale.

But he didn't need to feel that pain in his throat if he didn't want to. He didn't need to breathe, after all.

He stopped.

"Don't." Martin's tone was unreadable. Was he back to being disgusted? Afraid? Angry? All those things at once?

Robin couldn't reply without drawing breath, and if he did that it would mean Martin had won. Robin didn't want Martin to win. He didn't want anything from the fragile, breakable, living world to gain even the tiniest advantage over him ever again.

"So that's your solution? Just stop? Opt out of anything that holds the potential to hurt you?"

Robin shrugged.

"It's always worth it, you know. The pain that comes at the end; the loss when someone dies, or a relationship breaks up. Even when it hurts like hell, it's still worth it."

The words were so trite that Robin couldn't let them pass without remark, even if it did mean breathing in to speak. "You sound like a fucking greeting card."

"That doesn't mean I'm wrong."

"So what? Even if you're right, you're talking about what it feels like for a human. Of course it feels worth it for you! You can move on. The bad things that happen shape you. You're a part of a huge living fucking ecosystem. Even when it feels like your heart's ripped out it's still natural to you. It's how your world works. I don't change! I don't grow from my experiences! I don't grow at all! Things are never in the past for me. I'm exactly the same, every night!"

Martin was quiet for a long time as Robin stood there, chest heaving. Robin imagined that each of those heaving breaths must smell terrible, of blood and booze and kisses from a mouth that wasn't Martin's.

"I understand." Martin's words were calm. "This isn't about you wanting to cut yourself off from reality. It's the opposite. You're here because you felt disconnected from humans, and picking a fight with me would mean that you were getting attention from someone. Any attention would be good attention. What are you, an infant? That's an immensely shitty, fucked-up way of making yourself feel grounded and connected. It's at my expense."

Maybe Martin had a point. So? So what? What the hell did he know about anything?

"I used to feed on you. Waaaay before we got together," Robin confessed with a brittle chuckle. "I'd wipe alllll your memories of me and then meet you for the first time over and over and over again."

"Yeah, I know that, you dumb shit," snapped Martin. "I'm not fucking stupid. I put two and two together after you were so shocked it didn't take, that first night we went out. I was hoping you'd tell me in better circumstances than a pointless fight about nothing, though."

"It's not pointless!" Robin snapped right back. "I'm trying to make you see. Why won't you see that I don't deserve you? I was a soldier in a war so bad they thought it would end war forever! I've killed people! I'm a fucking vampire, for Christ's sake. It's not right. It's not fair. You make me so fucking happy. I don't deserve to be happy. I deserve to be alone. I don't want to be alone. But I should be."

"Do you actually want to be with me?" Martin asked. "Or is it just that you don't want to be alone?"

Robin stared at him, not really understanding the question. "What difference does it make? What difference does any goddamned thing make?"

"It makes a difference because..." Martin paused. "Because if you're just with me because you don't want to be alone, then fucking fine. Maybe you've done shitty things. Maybe you can't ever find a way to balance whatever abstract cosmic scale you've imagined up that needs to be put back into balance."

He drew a deep breath. "But if it's that you want to be with me, specifically, then fuck that whole idea. You think you don't deserve me? You think it isn't fair that you get to be this happy? Fine. Fucking fine. Life's not fair. Who gives a shit? I want to be with you. If you want to be with me, isn't that enough?"

Robin didn't know what to say to that; what would make Martin see that it was a nice dream, but that it wasn't true. It wasn't that simple. In the end, Robin just gave a quiet grunt, staring stubbornly at the ground.

Martin ran a hand through his own hair and shook his head. "I'm going to bed. You do what you like. I'm too old to stay up listening to tantrums."

Robin gave a broken bark of laughter, spreading his arms out wide. "Do you think I'm as old as I look? Honestly now. Did you think that just because I know how to text and dress like the students who come into your cafe, I'm truly eighteen?" It was so funny he had to laugh again. If he kept laughing, he wouldn't scream. "I'm more than a fucking century old! A hundred goddamn years! So don't you dare tell me that you're too old for anything. I'm too old for everything. I should be rotting in the ground. Or at the absolute best I should be shitting myself in some home, being spoon-fed apple sauce and wheeled out on Christmas so my great-grandchildren don't feel guilty about me. I should be..." His voice cracked. Robin dropped his arms to his sides, hanging his head. "I should be dead or alive, not stuck in the middle like this," he said quietly.

He couldn't look up at Martin. He couldn't stand to see the faint repulsion that would be there, as Martin finally understood just how wrong Robin was. He was a thing that shouldn't exist.

"We never would have met at all."

Martin's voice was quiet. After so much loud arguing, it was the softness of his words, their low volume that hit Robin like a blow. The sadness in them was too large to fit inside a shout; it could only be conveyed quietly.

"With either of those outcomes, we never would have met." Martin gave a hollow laugh. "If you think you're a selfish asshole...fuck, apparently we deserve each other, then, because I...I'm glad you're like this if that's true. Because I'm glad I met you. I hate the thought of a world where you died before I was born, and we never even glanced across each other's lives for a second. We would never have met, never have touched. I would rather you were a vampire, and here, than any other possible option."

Robin crumpled to the floor, like a puppet whose strings had all been sliced. He sat there, staring up at Martin, struggling to find words and discovering that he had none.

Martin knelt in front of him, reaching out to cradle his cheek in one palm. Robin just stared.

He should be furious. He should be murderously furious. How dare Martin say that? How dare he? How dare...

It wasn't until Martin hushed him that Robin realized he'd begun to cry in gulping, ugly little sobs. He lurched forward, clinging to Martin in an embrace that barely left the human room to breathe. Everything was wrong, and awful, and sad, but without those elements he wouldn't have Martin, either. It was all or nothing.

Right now, Robin was very, very grateful to have Martin. He let Martin hold him, their positions awkward but neither of them moving. They just stayed as they were, and Robin wept hopelessly into the fabric of Martin's faded shirt.

He wasn't even sure how to articulate, even to himself, what he was so upset about. Maybe it was just the alcohol, finding another way to turn him into an asshole. Maybe it had been seeing Ben. It could have been a lot of things. Robin had a smorgasbord of options, when it came to needing an excuse to cry. Which one of them had finally tipped him over into actually doing it, though, would probably stay a mystery.

Even so, it was...not nice, exactly, but freeing, to let the tears flow while resting in the safety of Martin's arms. Robin felt too heavy and weary to move, anyway, even if there had been somewhere else he'd rather be. Even his eyelids were tired. He...

Martin was gone when Robin woke up the next evening, and Robin climbed out of the bed feeling like he should be aching and sore and tired. The exemplary condition that vampire bodies remained in under almost all circumstances created severe cognitive dissonance when your brain told you that you should feel like absolute crap, and yet you didn't. If anyone had ever earned a hangover, it was him, but he was feeling fine.

He went to the bathroom and turned on the shower, and then realized that he had no idea whether Martin was working that night and, if so, how late.

How incredibly strange that lack of knowledge felt. Once upon a time, and a very recent time at that, Martin's schedule was the only thing that gave any sort of structure to Robin's week—what days he worked, and what time, and how long he needed to be able to sleep the next morning versus what time he had to wake up.

Somewhere in the last short span of days and weeks, Robin's time and attention had begun to fill with other things. There were other people who interested him; places and activities with no direct relationship with Martin's blood and how Robin could get it.

The realization was a strange one because at the same time Robin felt like his life now had Martin at the center of it in a way that his previous obsession hadn't had the capability for. How could a person be more important, and less vital, to him at the same time?

He showered and dressed, stealing some of Martin's clothes instead of putting his own cigarette-scented outfit of the night before back on. Martin's clothes were too large on him, but Robin decided that belting oversized jeans and turning up the hems was its own kind of waif chic, and baggy black T-shirts were a perennial staple of young people's wardrobes in this era, weren't they? He wouldn't look that weird.

It wasn't that Robin cared about fashion all that much, just that his hyperawareness of the need to blend in and be as unmemorable as possible was always present in his head. It wasn't the kind of habit he could break just because his clothes were in the wash.

Once he was dressed, Robin took Nora out for a walk. As usual, this involved her straining on the end of the leash as hard as she could pull, making her own breaths into little wheezing gasps from the pressure of the collar as she strove to go faster, faster.

"You know, all empirical evidence and your personal experience suggests that this is never, ever going to work," Robin pointed out to her conversationally. "And yet you always do it. Is it that your brain is a defective sultana, or that you're an optimist? Or a combination of the two?"

Nora's only reply was to bark threateningly at a passing senior citizen on a mobility scooter.

The fight the night before had ended in tears, rather than shouted attacks, but Robin didn't know if that meant things were all right between them or not now. Martin had said he was glad that Robin was in his life, but what if sleep and distance had changed his mind? What if, removed from the heat of the moment, Martin had realized that his life would be much better off without Robin in it?

And what would Robin do, he wondered to himself, if Martin never wanted to see him again?

Even thinking the question frightened him; he expected the abyss to yawn open at his feet, even darker and larger than it had been back in the days before he'd first caught sight of Martin. And yet, somehow, it didn't. Robin was still horrified by the thought of having to endure losing so much, especially as it was because of his own hideous, selfish, reckless idiocy, but he knew that even such a fate wouldn't make him want to go back to his room, to the same existence he'd had before. He wouldn't sit and let the dust pile up; let the days go by without acknowledgement. He would remain interested in the world, even if Martin was lost to him forever.

Robin wasn't quite sure when it was that this part of him had changed, but he was grateful it had. Solitude and apathy had become his own personal hell—one he had no power to save himself from.

By the time he got back to Martin's house, Nora's walk had been drawn out as long as it could be without exhausting her to the point where Robin would have to carry a wriggling, fractious dog under his arm all the way home.

Martin was sitting on his sofa. Nora jumped up beside him for the cuddles and pettings that she clearly considered to be her due. Martin paid her enough attention to calm her down and then maneuvered her out of the way so that Robin could lie against him if he wanted.

Robin could feel tight-wound coils of tension leave his shoulders between one instant and the next. "You don't want me to leave immediately and never come back?"

Martin shook his head but didn't quite manage a smile. "I don't want that, no. And...I can't tell you what to do. I don't know if what I'm about to say is even feasible. I have no idea what that part of your life is like. But, that said, I don't want you feeding off people and then taking their memories of it away afterwards. It sits badly with me. If you're worried that you can't find people who won't freak out, then just feed off me, okay?"

Robin made a small, doubtful sound. "I don't know. It's a very long time since I've encountered another vampire. We're not very common. It might be difficult to find a way to be put in touch with people who, as you put it, 'won't freak out.'"

"There should be a website where people can make profiles for this stuff. Everything would be way easier that way," Martin mused. Robin snorted.

"Yeah, I'll just set up an Internet dating profile so I can find willing victims whose blood I can drink. Then, when I get incredibly arrested and extremely dissected by science, my not-guilty plea will be 'it was my boyfriend's idea.'"

"Oh, please. So long as nobody winds up actually hurt, nobody would even look askance at a proposition like that. The Internet is a wild place."

"I may be remarkably bad at most social mores," said Robin. "But even I know that this is a terrible plan."

"Whatever. We'll work out the problem later. If you do need to keep doing things the way you've been taking care of it in the past, we'll..."

"We'll find a compromise," Robin assured him, finishing the thought. "I don't want to do something that makes you unhappy."

"Thank you."

Robin closed his eyes, breathing in Martin's warm, living scent. His interest in the world wouldn't have disappeared if he'd lost this, he knew that now, but that didn't mean he wasn't deeply, profoundly glad he didn't have to face a future without Martin. Not just yet.

"Are we okay?" he asked Martin, even though he was pretty sure he knew the answer. To hear the confirmation spoken would be a small extra comfort.

"Yeah," Martin answered; the word a sigh. "We're okay. I get that what happened with Ben left you really fucked up. We all have shit like that."

"Mm. I guess. I'll try not to be an enormous asshole about it, if I get blindsided by something that messes with my head," Robin said, his eyes still closed. He knew he should apologize outright, but the idea stuck in his throat a little bit.

It wasn't that he wasn't sorry—he was deeply, deeply sorry; regret like a tangible weight pressing down on him. But he felt as if saying so would present an impression that he somehow felt this regret was, in itself, sufficient penance for how he'd acted.

Rather than simply telling Martin how sorry he was, Robin intended to demonstrate the fact by changing how he behaved in the future, and making sure to avoid repeating his mistakes.

Martin stroked Robin's hair in a soothing, petting motion. "Do you want to talk about any of it?"

"Maybe. I don't know. I don't think so," Robin said. "But...I could tell you about how I died, if you want."

"Is it something you want to tell me?"

Robin thought about it. "Yeah...yeah, I think it is."

Robin sat up from where he lay against Martin, feeling a vague wish that Nora wasn't happily destroying a tennis ball piece by piece on the other end of the sofa. He wished she was near enough to hug, even though he was well aware that she was not and never had been a dog who was good at comforting. According to Martin, she typically ran away out of sight at the first sign of human distress.

That was sort of amusing, in fact: Robin, whose species was designed to be removed, remote, and without empathy, had somehow managed to entangle himself in the emotional wellbeing of several people, and rather than using this to his own personal advantage, he instead felt a great sense of personal distress and reciprocal reliance on them to look after his own heart. Meanwhile, Nora was a dog—creatures notorious for their empathy and caring; their loyalty even when the devotion came at the expense of their quality of life—and yet Nora was, well, Nora, who actively fled any situation where someone might want to draw comfort from her, and who demonstrably considered all love and affection it was possible to bestow upon her to be nothing but the baseline attention that the universe should feel obligated to provide her with.

Martin sure did have a knack for picking the defective ones.

"I haven't thought about any of this in a long time," Robin admitted to Martin, forcing his mind to abandon idle tangents and come back to the topic at hand. "It wasn't that I repressed them, or even tried especially hard to lock them away. I just...discouraged myself from examining or recalling them. There were reasons enough in my daily life to feel despair; I didn't have to venture back into the past for that. It was easier to avoid thinking, as much as possible."

"You don't have to talk about this if you don't want to."

"I know," Robin said. "But it isn't that I don't want to talk about it. It's crappy to talk about, but that's not the same thing."

He took a deep, ragged breath.

"So. I...I sort of died in the First World War."

"Sort of?" Martin asked gently.

"Yeah." Robin shrugged. He was still finding it difficult to look at Martin. Sitting beside him like this meant that Robin didn't have to. That made saying it all a little easier. "Sort of. I started dying in a field hospital and finished the job when I got back home to my family's farm. I've...I've never told anyone any of this. Sorry if it doesn't make sense right away."

"It's all right. Take your time."

"I signed up after my older brother died. He was...he's got a Wikipedia page, listed in the *World War One poets* category. He was famous even before he died, so you can imagine how crazy people went over his poems after he was gone. I'd just recently begun to try my hand at journalism, and every time I introduced myself people always said, 'Oh, you're Bert's brother,' as soon as they heard my name." Robin gave a small frown. "I was being held up against a ghost for comparison in everything I did. A perfect, talented ghost. I couldn't even resent him for it, because my sisters and my parents were so stricken over his loss, and I missed him so deeply myself. I'm sure you know yourself how complicated it feels to be angry at the dead."

"Yeah," Martin agreed with a soft sigh, holding Robin tighter with the arm across his shoulders, and drawing him closer in against his side. Martin was warm, and the heat that the student's blood had temporarily given Robin had long ago faded from his own skin. "I know."

The memory of his sisters made Robin tear up. "Look at me. It's stupid. Apart from Bert, my family had perfectly ordinary human lifespans. There's no reason for me to cry for them like this. They had their time, and then their time ended. It's the best anyone gets."

Martin's voice was slow and soft. "It's all right to miss the dead, Robin. It doesn't matter what the details were. It's still all right to miss them."

Robin gave a ragged sigh. "The actual story of how I became a vampire started away from home, as I said. I'd been injured, and found myself a patient in a field hospital. There was a nurse there...She was a vampire, and used false papers to infiltrate the enemy's side. It was actually quite clever, really. A way to use her predatory nature for a patriotic cause. And I suppose it's stupid to call them false papers." Robin's scoffing sound was almost soundless and without amusement. "All our papers are false. Her papers for her own country would have been just as fake as any other she had, unless she was newly changed enough to pass for the age she would have been if she was alive."

He thought of Polly again, for a moment. He hoped that she'd never look so much younger than her actual age that people thought she was a liar. It had been a horrible day when Robin had realized he'd no longer be able to convince anyone that he was simply stunted and baby-faced; that he'd have to leave his identity behind and start again.

"The nurse was feeding off enemy troops. She was killing them, which vampires almost never do under ordinary circumstances. The death toll was hidden by the general carnage, of course. It was like...no. Nothing is like war. Nothing." Robin shivered at the memories he'd carried in his head for so many years. Then he shrugged, forcing himself to return to the particulars of his origin. "And then one night, it was my turn to fall prey to her."

He sat up a little straighter. He didn't want the feeling of Martin's warmth associated with these memories in any way. "I was weak, and injured. Who knows, maybe I would have died anyway, under the natural progression of things. There's no way to know one way or the other, now. She bit me and drank from me, and though I didn't quite understand what was happening to me,

I could still tell that something terrible was going on."

Robin's hands were shaking. He rubbed them against his thighs, trying to hide the tremor. "She was careless. Too caught up in draining me dry to notice how I was clawing at her arms, trying to shove her away. It's amazing, the reserves of strength we sometimes find when we're fighting for our lives. My nails were blunt, but I was still able to scratch at her enough to draw blood. And once I had done that..."

The tremors in his hands and the shiver in his spine became a full-bodied shudder. Robin could hear the chatter of his own teeth. "The smell of vampire blood is very powerful for someone drained almost to the point of death. Every other sense narrowed and dimmed, beside the strength of that scent. I no longer cared if I died, so long as I could taste that blood before I went."

He swallowed; a phantom of that first hunger in his throat. It made him feel ill. "I'm sure you can see exactly how it goes from there. I managed to swallow enough of it to survive her attack. When she realized what I was doing, it made her laugh and laugh. She must have felt at least a little of the things that I came to feel, and so she knew I was damning myself to something far worse than simple death."

Robin didn't want to talk about the specific processes involved in his change from human to vampire. The thought of describing it even briefly made him feel sick, as if he was approaching a yawning, dark pit, and every instinct was telling him to run. That there was a darkness down there he could not look at and survive the experience.

The hairs on the back of his neck actually began to prickle; standing up at the memory of the threat, at the thought of having to revisit that memory again.

Robin swallowed and steadied his hands, rubbing his palms against his thighs. Martin didn't say anything and didn't try to touch him. Robin was so grateful for that. When all this was done and he'd finished the story, he would want Martin to hold him again. But not while he was telling it. Not while he was remembering.

His voice was, to his own ears, shockingly composed as he began talking again, as if he was recounting something he had heard secondhand, or read about in a book.

"My health began to improve at once after that, of course. It seemed as if I'd turned a corner in my recovery; all my wounds were healing quickly and cleanly. I was on my way home almost before I knew it and assumed that I was as healthy and whole as I appeared to be.

"Then my heart began to stumble. The stubborn will to live that had kept it alive through that first attack was being worn thin by the blood I'd taken from her. Isn't that ironic? Caring so much, refusing to die, is what left me trapped in this limbo world of apathy. Isn't that hideously, horrifically ironic?"

"You can't have always been like that, though," Martin said. "All those languages you know...you must have still had enthusiasm about the world when you were traveling."

"Yes. It wasn't becoming a vampire that made me this way, not immediately. It was the slow realization that I could love the world utterly, but that didn't mean I could ever really be a part of it again. No amount of travel and reading and museums and art galleries could stop my sisters growing into adult women, becoming mothers and then grandmothers, while I stayed as unchanging as a photograph. I could learn every language in the world, but the mouth I use to speak them would still be the fanged maw of a monster."

"But..." Martin's forehead was furrowed in a worried frown. "Look, I'm not belittling what you've been through, because frankly I think I'd be just as miserable as you are about the whole thing, if it were me. You got dealt a massively shitty hand by the universe. I don't think you should write yourself off as being beyond help, though. Not yet. Lots of other people get dealt shitty hands, too, of various kinds."

"I don't think they make antidepressants for vampires."

"Put the wisecracks to the side, and try actually listening to me instead. Garbage luck happens to a lot of people, and they find a way to cope with it. That doesn't mean it doesn't suck. It doesn't mean their lives are perfect. It's not fair, and it doesn't start being fair just because you decide not to give up anymore." Martin shrugged. "All I'm saying is: yeah, you're right. You could do a thousand amazing things, and you'd still be a vampire at the end of them. But isn't doing a thousand amazing things better than not doing them if that's how it turns out at the end either way?"

Despite himself, Robin smirked. "This sounds suspiciously like another way of phrasing your 'love is always worth it' thing from our argument, you know."

Martin had the good grace to look guilty at having been caught out. "Well...it's true, isn't it? If I'm going to be dead less than a hundred years from now, whether you're willing to share your time with me or not, then shouldn't simple logic tell you that it's better to take the opportunity?"

"I don't think you quite comprehend how lonely it can be, to be outside the cycles of life and seasons." Robin's voice was quiet.

"I'll never know what it's like to experience, no," Martin conceded. "But...forever is a very long time, Robin. I hate the idea of you spending it alone."

Robin didn't know what to say to that, so he kissed Martin instead. It was a fervent, near-desperate kiss, because Robin wasn't simply trying to make Martin feel good, or to feel good himself—he was trying to convey by gesture all the things he didn't know how to explain with words.

Martin kissed him back, softly and slowly, forcing Robin to reduce his own intensity. Soon the pace between them was calm and quiet. For the first few minutes Robin was half afraid that Martin would be too gentle with him, like when he'd practically killed Robin with kindness by forcing him to be the helpless recipient of care. But Martin didn't try anything like that this time. Perhaps he could tell that Robin was too wrung out, too spent, for anything but the simplest kinds of affection.

They moved from the sofa to the bed after a while, Robin's exhaustion transformed into kiss-drunk lust. His skin ached to be touched by Martin's. He needed to feel the intimacy of the two of them together; he needed it as soon as possible.

The sex itself, Martin sliding into Robin's body as if the two of them had been designed for one another, was both unimportant and vitally important all at once. Robin felt as if he was a prism, refracting broken rays of light in every color, the scattered shades each one part of the single whole. Red for the quiet intimacy between them; gold for the trust they placed in one another; green for sweet, wicked touches; blue for Robin's hand clenching at the sheets as he cried out softly, his legs shaking with the intensity of the pleasure he felt; violet for the two of them entwined together as climax washed over them, Martin capturing Robin's lips with his own and swallowing the high whine from Robin's mouth.

He felt so warm. He felt so loved. It was like being out in direct sunshine. It was like being alive.

☆☆☆

Robin lay awake for a long time afterward, confusion keeping his mind ticking long after Martin's breaths had evened and slowed. He just couldn't understand. How was it that, even after the story of Robin's ending and beginning, even after their vicious argument, Martin wanted to be here beside him, holding Robin in his arms? How was it that Martin didn't hate him?

The hours passed slowly, offering no answer to the riddle.

"How can it be," Robin asked, keeping his voice hushed enough that it wouldn't disturb Martin's slumber, "that you see me for what I really am, you know me for who I really am...and you're still here?"

Perhaps it was impossible to solve the mystery. He'd have to just accept that, against all common sense, Martin cared about him. He'd have to try and be worthy of that caring, whether he understood it or not.

Robin moved closer, pressing himself to Martin's chest. He could hear the man's heartbeat, a slow and steady pulse that grounded Robin, lulling him down toward elusive rest.

Being cared about, as strange and wonderful as it was, didn't make the rest of Robin's existence suddenly perfect. There was still so much in him that was jagged or cold or numb; brittle edges and dark, sucking bogs that he might never be ready to think about sufficiently to deal with. He knew better than anyone what a mess he was.

But it was something. It was a start. And it made the rest seem less daunting, if only slightly.

Chapter Eight

Martin

Sarah was, by and large, an extremely dependable and responsible kind of person. She did have a wild streak to her, however, and had done so for as long as Martin had known her. These days, that wild streak tended to take the form of Sarah occasionally making huge decisions completely out of the blue, like deciding to sell all her furniture and completely change the look of her home, or getting the time and date of Polly's birth tattooed on her arm.

So Martin, while surprised, was at the same time not in the least shocked when Sarah rang at an extremely late hour in the night and announced to him that she was planning on taking Polly on a theme-park vacation as soon as possible.

"I want her to have one last big, amazing memory of doing kid stuff," Sarah explained to Martin. "Before it's too late. Pol's growing up so fast, you know? And she never got to do nearly enough kid stuff because she was ill so much. This is the last chance."

Knowing that "as soon as possible," when Sarah was in this mood, literally meant "as quickly as I can pack the car," Martin just grinned to himself and told her he was going to transfer to her as much money as she was willing to accept from him—much less than he wanted to offer; much more than she wanted to take—and then, once he'd said good-bye to her and hung up the phone, started planning ways that he could make sure that his staff would always be free to take time off to live their life when they needed to.

For Sarah, Martin would have encouraged her to go regardless of the circumstances at the shop, but now that he was thinking about it, he wanted to be certain that anyone could do it when required. A job should help people, not hinder them.

When the solution to the staffing dilemma came to him, Martin almost smacked himself on the forehead for taking so long to think of it, because once he'd thought of it, it seemed like the most obvious and natural thing.

He was writing down notes on how to go about it, planning tentative schedules, when Robin woke up from a very long sleep-in and shuffled out of the bedroom.

"You're hiring Ben?" he asked Martin, reading the plans over his shoulder.

"And a few others, if I can," Martin replied. "But yes, Ben's the one that I'm keen to get. It'll stop him from getting too isolated again. Everyone needs friends."

"I used to think I didn't," Robin admitted in a quiet voice, sounding rueful. Martin pulled him down for a brief brush of lips, wishing there was a way to convey how much he wished he could take away some of Robin's unhappiness and carry it himself.

Robin sat down opposite Martin at the table. "I'm considering killing off my current identity."

"What?"

"It's about time to refresh the alias I keep as an emergency backup; I might as well get some use from it before I dispose of it. Remind me to make sure Lauren Edwards at the bank is remembered fondly by my estate, because she really did put up with a lot from cranky old Mr. St John." Robin laughed softly to himself. "Once I'm set up under the other name, I'll hire a cleaning firm to completely empty out my apartment and rent it. I'll stay in hotels for a while. I've done that before. It helps me properly feel like I've stopped being my old self, and I can start adjusting to the new."

"Do you ever struggle with it? Making up new people to be, I mean."

"Not really," Robin replied. "I'm well-practiced at it now. Remember, I haven't been able to be myself in a century. Apart from when I'm with you."

The words of the last sentence were thrown out offhandedly as if Robin didn't even realize the weight and importance of them. Looking at him, in the silence that hung in the air after they'd been said, Martin suspected Robin did know, but he found it easier to pretend he didn't. Martin decided to let the sentiment pass without remark, even if it did make something inside his own chest feel warm and bright to hear it.

"You can stay here instead of a hotel," he told Robin. "If you want. You're here practically every night anyway, and we know that you can sleep here without the sun being too much for you."

"If I do that, Martin, it'll be hard for me to think up a new identity that belongs anywhere but here."

"Is that so bad?"

Robin gave him a rueful smile. "Yes, unfortunately. For your sake, I want to be a fully created individual, not a half-formed acolyte who exists for no real other reason but to watch you obsessively and consider methods by which I might contrive to make my life intersect with yours."

"Well, when you put it like that, I see your point," Martin replied with a grin. Sometimes Robin's florid wordiness was downright adorable. "Hey, change of subject for a minute. You know how to use the Internet, right?"

Robin made a scoffing sound. "No. I only use an abacus and

carrier pigeons, and sometimes Morse code if I'm feeling modern. Of course I do; only being able to go to stores after dark made shopping quite difficult before everything was available online. And sometimes I feel like reading newspapers or watching something. Not often, but sometimes."

"Everyone does that stuff online. I meant using it for putting out information, as well as getting it," Martin specified. "Do you have any social media profiles?"

"No. There aren't exactly any class reunions for me to get invited to, so what's the point?"

"Does it ever get exhausting, being spiky and flippant about everything? Sure, you might be right about not being able to reconnect with people you knew when you were alive, but there's lots of people you know now that you could keep in touch with. Me, Polly and Sarah, Ben."

"Wow, I know a whole four people."

"I could always set up a page for Nora. That'd make it five," Martin offered. That earned a snort of laughter from Robin.

"Okay, deal. If you make your dog a profile, I'll make myself one."

"You could set up a blog, too." Martin kept his tone as light and idle as he could, hoping that he could offer the suggestion without immediately scaring Robin off the whole idea. "Maybe write about the war. Even write about being a vampire, if you want—it's the Internet, so it's hardly the weirdest thing anyone will have seen. They'll just chalk it up to role-play or metaphor and move on."

"Mm." The sound was noncommittal, but it also wasn't an outright denial, and Martin felt that it was at least a partial victory.

☆☆☆

Here's something I've learned after a hundred years of being around: daily routines don't stop even when the context turns awful. Life doesn't stop, but at the same time it feels as if life has stopped, at least inside you.

This is the best way I can try to explain what it's like to be a vampire: you still walk the same streets, see the same sights, and yet the things that were inside you have been replaced with nothing but an empty howling.

Over the years, I've been told multiple times (by humans, who have never known what it is to look at their future and see nothing but pain and darkness, forever, staring back; and by other vampires, the ones who claim to have somehow overcome the despair that this fate carries with it) that it's possible to learn ways of coping with that howl. Until very recently, I never believed them for a moment.

I'm not sure if I believe them yet, even now, but I'm willing to entertain the notion. It's only a first step, but someone very close to me says that there is never anything "only" about first steps.

☆☆☆

"I've been getting emails from a bunch of people, about the blog," Robin told Martin, a few weeks later. "You were right, by the way. Nobody gives a damn about the vampire thing. I've had a couple of people actually call it a 'clever gimmick'."

"Told you so."

"And one of them emailed me the link to a thread on a message board, where everyone had decided to find out who the 'real' guy writing the entries was, and if the man I was 'claiming' to be from the war had ever really existed."

"Hmm? What did they find?"

Robin stretched his hands above his head and then pillowed his head on his hands. "That the domain name was registered to the great-grandson of the original soldier, of course. I'm meticulous about things like that."

"You're meticulous about everything. One might even say fastidious."

"Yeah, yeah," Robin said breezily, blithe in the face of Martin's gentle teasing. "Most of the messages have been from readers who want me to know that they appreciate the way I'm using vampirism as a metaphor for depression. One girl even wants to write a paper on me for her university class. Frankly, it just makes me wonder if there's anything vampirism can't be used as a metaphor for, considering the variety of things I've seen attributed to it over the years."

☆☆☆

I've been thinking about studying something. It seems a waste to exist in a time and place where night school is available, and not take advantage of the fact that I'd be able to painlessly attend classes.

Every time I give the notion serious thought I get overwhelmed, though. Before I could even get as far as deciding on what subject I'd like to learn about, I'd have to work hard at learning how students of this day and age think and talk.

I watch them in coffee shops, and they're so at ease with themselves and their place in the world. Can something like that be mimicked properly? That surety you are a part of the wanted world, rather than a monster trying to blend in amongst the crowd?

☆☆☆

"That entry's getting a lot of compliments for its metaphor, too," Robin told Martin. "Apparently I'm talking about minority groups who 'pass' as part of the mainstream when they're in public, and the uneasiness of their identities. See, what did I tell you? Vampires can be a metaphor for anything."

"Do you have a favorite?"

"A favorite metaphor?"

"Yeah," Martin confirmed, nodding. "Is there one that you prefer for your readers to assume you're using?"

Robin looked thoughtful. "Lately, I've begun to think it's all right for it to mean more than one thing. After all, I used to think that I was one thing and one thing only, and you...you made me feel like I was more than that. I'm only one vampire, and there are lots of others out there, somewhere. Some of them must feel even more like they're only one thing, or another. Being a vampire has to encompass all those different single elements that they want to define themselves by. It has to mean everything that people need it to mean."

Robin paused for a moment, worrying his lower lip between his teeth for a moment before he went on. "But...if I had to pick one single metaphor, to encompass what the blog has taught me about what being a vampire means, it would be that those who dwell in coffins aren't alive, not really. Obviously that's phrased incredibly awkwardly, because I'm formulating this while I'm talking right now..." He gave an awkward laugh. "But, well, my point is that nobody can thrive while they're in a tomb, just by the nature of where they are. The only way to be alive is to be a part of the living world. And I didn't learn that from writing the blog, not really. I learned it from you. From loving you. From being loved by you."

Suddenly, his face brightened into a grin. "Hey, what's your favorite restaurant? Let's go there. As a celebration of my social media popularity."

"A restaurant? Wouldn't it make more sense to go somewhere that we'll both enjoy?"

"No. Restaurant. Let me know where, and I'll make a

reservation for later this week," Robin declared decisively.

Which was why, a few nights later, the pair of them sat down together at a table in a small Italian restaurant Martin had been visiting for years. It was a small, charming place: the warm, dim air rich with garlic and onion and parmesan smells; the walls painted in soft red and plum shades. It was one of the few locations, apart from The Warm Taste and his home, where Martin felt safe and at ease. And yet...

"I'm still not sure why you picked somewhere with food as your celebration outing," Martin said to Robin. "I appreciate the gesture, but it seems unfair."

"It's a place you like. Making you happy makes me happy," Robin answered. Martin must have looked dubious about the response, because Robin's smile skewed into something slightly more cynical. "I feed off humans, remember. If you're having a great time, I can leech that off and have a good one myself."

That reply just made Martin even more skeptical. "You're not that kind of vampire. Trust me, you're so much more benign than people I've known who operate like that. They don't go out of their way to make people happy so that they can be happy as well. They just choose a victim, latch on, and suck 'em dry. No need for fangs or blood; ordinary humans are more than equipped for that kind of thing."

"All right, you got me," Robin admitted. "Aside from making you happy—which is a real and legitimate motive on my part!—I picked a restaurant because I'm going to try to have dinner with you. Nothing too fancy. But I'll give it a shot."

Martin looked very confused. "What, you mean...food? Can you even do that?"

Robin shrugged. "Depends. I guess we'll see."

Martin ordered a small simple pizza with cheese and tomato slices and tomato paste. He'd had enough different tiers of pizza over the years—chewy, cheap slices bought in paper bags from cafes along the boulevard; standard chain-store delivery pies ordered by selection off websites; the delicious concoctions offered at this restaurant—to know that the better quality the pizza expected, the simpler the selection of ingredients should be.

"I think that's why not many of our patrons order the complicated, extra-flavored kinds of coffee," Martin went on, after he'd explained his pizza-evaluating wisdom to Robin. "Some of them do, and we're happy to make it of course, but they're not as popular at The Warm Taste as they are at other places, and I think that's because I always get the best-grade beans and milk I can. It's worth it."

Robin gave him a soft smile. "You're cute when you're passionate. Granted, you're cute all the time, but especially when you're passionate."

"Incorrect—I am distinguished and mature. You're meant to be the cute one," Martin corrected. "We might as well accept the roles Sarah's cast us in."

Robin snorted. "If only she knew that you're the twink here, really."

Robin's order was beef broth pasta and a glass of red wine. He managed a few spoonfuls of the broth, sipping it thoughtfully. His expression was curious, rather than revolted, which Martin thought was a good sign.

Then Robin speared one of the curls of pasta and brought it to his mouth. There was such trepidation in the entire sequence of actions that Martin couldn't help but laugh a little.

Robin chewed for a long time and then swallowed. He made a face, squeezing his eyes shut for a few seconds.

"Forgotten what solids are like?" Martin guessed. Robin nodded.

"It's not bad, it's just...I might need to get used to them over time." He drank some of the wine instead. "But I'll keep trying."

✩✩✩

After dinner they walked back to Martin's place and sat together on the step at the back door, enjoying the night air and each other's company.

"Lately I've found myself smiling at the stars. That's a new experience for me. I'm not frightened of the universe at the moment," confessed Robin. "I used to be terrified of it, you know. Probably I will be again, someday in the future. But right now I'm not. I can look up at the night sky without thinking obsessively about the possibility that I'll live long enough to look up one night and remember a time when the stars were completely different."

"I hope you stay chill with the universe for long enough that you try tourism space travel when it gets invented," Martin said. "Sorry, I know you were being existential, but seriously, it would be such a bummer to be too freaked out by the concept of infinity to explore what's out there."

Robin laughed, resting his head on Martin's shoulder. "I hope it's soon enough that you can come with me."

"I bet you twinks say that to all the sugar daddies," Martin replied.

When the temperature dropped low enough that Martin started to feel uncomfortable staying outside, the two of them left the night sky behind them and went into Martin's bedroom, instead.

Spurred on by Robin having been game enough to try food at the restaurant, Martin decided it was time to tackle something that had been looming large in his own mind.

He drew a deep breath. He'd have to bring it up eventually, after all, and right then seemed as good a time as any.

"I think you should bite me."

Robin stared at him.

"We shouldn't be edging around it," Martin continued. "We can talk about it, and probably should, instead of just sliding up to it sideways. You know?"

"I don't know..." Robin's apprehension was practically palpable in the room. "Is this something you really want me to do to you, or something you just think you're meant to want me to do to you?"

Martin snorted. "Where would I be getting societal pressure from, exactly?"

"I don't know, films and novels and things." Shrugging uncomfortably, Robin looked away, rubbing the back of his own neck. "I don't want you to think that you have to do it or anything. When I used to do it to you...you're right, it was a shitty thing for me to do to a person. To you. I feel like it's sort of fucked up to take us back to something I did to you against your will. Without your will. However you want to define something like that."

"But do you want to bite me?"

"That's not relevant."

"It's completely relevant."

Robin threw his hands up, clearly frustrated. "Yes! Of course I do! Happy?"

"So what's the issue?"

"Ugh, you're impossible." Robin scowled. "Fine. Fine. Let's go."

"Really?"

"Sure. When you never want to look at me again, it's your own fault."

Robin's voice was an angry mutter, and he wouldn't look at Martin. Martin cupped his cheek with one hand and waited until Robin looked at him and their eyes met.

"That is never going to happen. All right? Never. And we don't have to do this if the thought of it worries you that much. But I want it, and you do, too. So let's be brave."

Robin screwed his eyes shut and drew in a deep breath. Then he nodded. "Okay."

Martin kissed him. "Okay."

Robin's touch was tentative and light as he guided Martin to sit on the edge of the bed. "Here, like this. And I'll—" He straddled Martin's lap, knees either side of Martin's thighs. The position made Robin taller than Martin, and Robin cupped the back of his head as they kissed. Martin let himself get used to the reversal of positions and found he rather liked what it felt like when Robin took the lead.

Robin kissed him until his lips were sensitive and tingling, claiming his mouth so unrelentingly that Martin felt a little dizzy—he couldn't properly catch his breath between the slick thrusts of Robin's tongue.

Tangling a hand in Martin's hair, making movement impossible, Robin moved his mouth away from Martin's own and sucked a quick hickey against Martin's throat. The move made Martin's head spin even more, and he placed his hands on Robin's hips so he'd have something to steady himself, a way to feel more grounded. Another hickey, lower and harder than the first, and then, before Martin even had a chance to moan, Robin struck.

The sting of the bite jolted every nerve in Martin's body into high, confused alert, as if he didn't know whether to protect himself from danger or hope desperately for more. The pace of his breathing quickened, his pulse thrumming. Robin's tongue lapped small strokes against the cut, collecting the beading blood that welled up each time.

Then he stopped and murmured quietly against Martin's skin, his lips brushing the wound with each word. "Sorry, habit. It'll be better if I..." He fastened his mouth to the bite and sucked.

The sensation was a hundred, a thousand times more intense than it had been a moment earlier. Martin could understand how, under other circumstances, a vampire's prey stayed still long enough to be drained dry—even the threat of death wouldn't be enough to make him want this to stop.

Robin's tongue pushed hard against the cut, the sudden sensation so sharply arousing that Martin pulled Robin even closer to him with a clumsy tug of his hands on Robin's hips. Robin moved one of his own hands down to lace his fingers with Martin's own, the pair of them holding tight to one another, a singular circulatory system with two hearts.

Martin lost his sense of time after a little while, the whole world narrowing down to Robin's mouth against his skin. When that feeling disappeared, Martin couldn't stop himself making a low groan.

"No, more, please."

"Shhh, it's all right. That's enough for now," Robin said gently. "Here, you lie here. I'll get you an orange juice."

Martin did as he was told, his mind a blank and pleasant haze. Robin returned, drink in hand, and wouldn't let Martin put it down until he drank every drop. The juice was cool and sweet, and when the glass was empty, Robin let him lie down again and climbed in beside him.

It was maybe forty minutes or an hour later before Martin properly came back to himself. When he did, he rolled over to face Robin in the bed.

"See? Still here."

At first, Robin's only reply was a tight, nervous smile. After a few minutes, when he saw that Martin really had been telling the truth and didn't seem to be going anywhere, he moved closer to him.

They lay together, their skin touching at random places all the way up and down the length of their bodies.

"Sorry that I'm so surprised. It's just...it's so novel," Robin mused, tracing idle patterns with his fingertip up and down Martin's forearm as they lay close. "To be with someone who doesn't mind what I am. Who can love even this."

"Yes," said Martin softly, catching Robin's hand up with his own. It was warmer than it had ever felt in the past.

Robin gave him a small, sad frown. "There isn't anything about you that's hard to love, Martin. That your parents ever made you think there was..." He shook his head, trailing off. "There isn't."

"I feel the same way, though," Martin told Robin, staring at him earnestly. "I know you think you're a monster, but I don't love you *despite* what you are. I love you. It's as simple as that. I don't divide you up into lovable and unlovable parts in my head. I love it all. I even love all the awful things we've each gone through. I love all our scars. Because they brought us here, to each other."

Robin pushed at Martin's shoulder with absolute gentleness. "Roll onto your stomach for a moment."

Martin complied. Robin's lips—so unfamiliarly warm, their temporary temperature changing the experience of their touch against Martin's skin completely—pressed gently against Martin's shoulder blade, kissing the place where a long, thin scar from a caning marked the flesh. Then Robin moved a little, over to the next marred spot, and kissed Martin's back again.

Slowly, with a tender reverence, Robin placed his lips to each of Martin's scars. Martin lay there, arms pillowing his head, until Robin was finished.

"I hate the pain you went through," Robin told him. "But I'm grateful for the man you became through enduring it."

Martin rolled back over onto his side, facing Robin, and took Robin's face in his hands, kissing him softly. "You'll have to tell me where your body's haunted places are, because the marks aren't ones that I can see."

Robin blinked hard at the words, and Martin could see that his eyes had grown bright with unshed tears. The phrasing must have meant a lot to him; the acknowledgement that invisible scars were no less real than the kind on Martin's back.

☆☆☆

When morning came, Martin left Robin sleeping in a nest of blankets and pillows, not much more than a pale blond shock of hair visible above the comforter.

Martin had bought more books about dogs than he'd ever need, back when he first got Nora. One of the books had mentioned that carnivores needed more sleep than other animals. He wondered if that played a role in the way that Robin slept for much more of each twenty-four-hour cycle than Martin did, or if the reason for Robin's rhythms was simply that his body clock worked on a scale so vast that each waking period was shorter just to keep Robin from being overwhelmed in the short term. Or what counted as short term for him, at least.

Martin wondered if Robin kept track of his family tree. He'd mentioned sisters—were their descendants still alive? Did he have cousins, second cousins; people out in the world who even now carried the genes and features that Robin had been born with?

If Robin didn't already know about what had become of the family he'd had when he was alive, maybe he'd like to find out. Maybe it was something that Martin could help him research someday. Martin wouldn't push him. One step at a time was enough. One night at a time.

Nora was destroying a plastic ball, shredding it into small pieces and eating them one by one. Martin had long ago stopped being shocked at the wide variety of non-foodstuffs his horrible dog would cheerfully consume. About the only thing that still confounded him was her love of raisin toast. She adored it, and every time he ate it, she would whine and beg beside his chair until he gave her the crusts.

Martin checked the day's mail. There was a postcard from Sarah, the glossy side showing a very blue sky and white-capped blue water, deeper and richer than the sky above it. The beach that ran along the bottom edge was a perfect golden yellow.

The blank side of the card was crammed edge to edge with Sarah's exuberant, messy handwriting, recounting fabulous views and amazing experiences, the word "awesome" appearing with heartening regularity. She also made mention that some of their plans had to be cancelled, which Martin assumed was because of Polly's unreliable stamina. But Sarah and Polly would both be used to that, having gone through it often enough that the disappointments wouldn't sting either of them too badly anymore.

If there was one fact all of them knew extremely well, it was that things could still be wonderful without being perfect. And it sounded like Polly and Sarah were having a wonderful holiday.

☆☆☆

It was over a week later before Martin found an opportunity that felt appropriate to raise the subject of Robin's original family. They were walking together, Nora having been left at home for a change so they could actually have some calm and quiet as they enjoyed the neighborhood.

After Martin asked how much, if anything, Robin knew about the topic, Robin was quiet for half a block's slow pace before replying.

"One of my sisters had five children," he said to Martin, his voice soft. "Her husband was competent enough, though he never appreciated her like she deserved. She died at thirty-seven, giving birth to the last two of her babies. The more robust of the twins lived through infancy. Grew up to look very like her mother."

"Did you keep track of her life, too?"

"Only as much as I had to in order to make sure she always had money when she was in need of it." Robin shook his head. "I know you mean well, and I appreciate the thought, but don't ask me to go down that path. If I stay tethered to my human past, I'll be swallowed by the weight of all the years since then that I've spent in the cold and dark. I have to build truly new lives for each of my reinventions. It's the only way I endure. I can't go back."

Martin held Robin's hand for the rest of the walk, neither of them saying anything.

When they got to the house, Martin got to work in the kitchen, rinsing out a small mixing bowl before measuring out a cup of butter, a cup of white sugar, and a cup of brown sugar. He worked them into a paste with uniform consistency, and then broke an egg into a teacup before pouring it into the mixing bowl.

"Well that doesn't look disgusting at all," Robin remarked, looking at the currently rather unappetizing beginnings of a batter that Martin was creating. "What's it going to be?"

"Cookies."

"What's the occasion?"

"Sarah and Polly are back from their trip. Polly emailed me as soon as they were home, declaring that she's coming over with movies she's determined to make me watch, so she's invited herself over for tomorrow evening. Apparently I'm unfit to be in her presence until I've seen *Spirited Away*. I pointed out to her that *Spirited Away* wasn't any newer than *Lilo and Stitch*, which she'd declared to be old, but she informed me that 'time counts different with anime.'"

Robin nodded with an overly sage and thoughtful expression. "She's clearly very wise. In cartoon-related theoretical physics concerning linear time, no less."

"Exactly. So I'm making a batch of chocolate chip cookies for us to eat while she teaches me."

Martin cracked the second egg into the teacup, checked it for stray shell fragments and other problems, and then began beating it into the mixture of other ingredients. "Pass me the vanilla?"

Robin reached over and snagged the bottle of extract. He handed it to Martin, who added a couple of teaspoons of it to the batter.

While he worked, Martin spoke. "I've been wondering about this for a while. Can you be sustained on human food? Or only on blood?"

"Only blood," Robin answered. "Unless there's a social reason—like going out to dinner with you—I never bother with human food, or even drinks."

"So all those coffees you bought, that was just so you had an excuse to stay in The Warm Taste and watch me?" Having put the mixing bowl aside, Martin dissolved a teaspoon of baking soda into hot water.

Robin smirked at him. "Yeah, yeah, you big egotist. Happy? I had a crush on you. I still have a crush on you."

Martin paused in his work, placing all the in-progress pieces on the countertop and temporarily ignoring them, deciding that a brief break for kissing Robin was very much necessary. The pace was slow and lazy, Martin's arms resting either side of Robin's head, as close to hugging as he could manage without touching Robin with his slightly baking-sticky hands. "But things like dinner, they don't harm you, do they?" he asked, mouth so close to Robin's that their lips brushed on some syllables.

"No. I've had to a few times in the past, to convince people I'm human, and it's never made me sick. I get out of the habit, so it's weird, but that's all."

"Does it taste all right?"

Robin's shoulders shrugged, Martin's arms still resting on them. "I suppose. I don't think it tasted any different to how it was when I was alive. I just don't have any reason to bother with it most of the time."

"Hmm." With one final kiss, Martin moved away to return to the ingredients he'd abandoned. He added the baking soda and half a teaspoon of salt to the mixing bowl and then followed those with three cups of flour and two cups of white chocolate chips. Sometimes Polly got a mild reaction to dark or milk chocolate, and so Martin figured it was better to be safe than sorry. Nobody needed hives interrupting their movie-watching afternoon.

"Can you put foil on those trays there?" he asked Robin as he stirred. Robin nodded, jumping down off the countertop to get the foil out of the drawer.

Martin took a moment to absorb the fact that he was getting kitchen help from an ageless, bloodthirsty vampire and grinned to himself at the perfect absurdity of it.

While the cookies spent ten minutes in the oven, going from dough to something that actually had form and solid texture, Martin cleaned up the kitchen. Or attempted to, anyway. Mostly he just made out some more with Robin, which was a more worthwhile use of his time than washing utensils.

When the timer went off, Martin got the batch out of the oven and left them on the counter to cool. This time, he actually did use the wait to clean up the kitchen, while Robin chatted to him and wasn't much use at all, sitting on the countertop again and observing.

"All right, I think these are ready," Martin declared, picking up one of the cookies. It was still warm; the chocolate a melted, gooey mess inside the baked crust. He broke off a small piece. "Open wide."

Robin hesitated for a beat, looking unsure, and then dutifully opened his mouth. Martin popped the piece of cookie inside Robin's mouth. "There."

Robin's whole face bloomed, his eyes opening wide and his eyebrows going up in surprise. An automatic, subconscious smile spread on his face.

Martin had learned how to tell the difference between the smiles Robin gave because he thought it was the correct moment in an interaction to offer a smile and the smiles Robin gave because he was so happy in that moment that he couldn't help but be smiling. This was definitely the second kind.

There was a wonderment in the smile, like Robin was remembering something he'd forgotten for a long time. He looked like he was being nourished, after existing on nothing but mere sustenance for so long he forgot there was anything else.

"You said that you don't have a reason to bother with food," Martin said. "But nobody has a reason to bother with cookies. That's not the point of cookies."

Robin just continued to grin and kissed Martin, smile and sweetness all bound up in the press of his lips.

☆☆☆

The next evening, as promised, Polly visited with a pile of movies.

"I even brought some ones I loved when I was little, since you love old stuff," she declared, brandishing a copy of *Ratatouille* as she spoke. "We don't have to watch everything today; I'll leave the rest behind for you to look at later."

"I feel like there's going to be an exam at the end," Martin joked. Polly's mouth twitched into a smile for a moment before she forced it back into seriousness.

"I'm just educating you. I'm giving you culture. Here, I'll even start with one that it'll be easy for you to like—it's about a girl who wants to own a restaurant." Polly opened one of the cases and popped out the disc, loading it into the player. "*The Princess and the Frog*. Robin, you have to watch too. It'll be your job to make sure Martin pays attention."

They all sat on the sofa, Polly on Martin's right side and Robin on his left, with Nora jumping up to join them by sprawling across Polly's lap a few moments later.

A wave of contentment swept over Martin; a sense that things were all exactly as they were meant to be. Even in his happiest of moments in the past, there had never been a feeling like this—a certainty that he had built himself exactly the life he wanted, full of the unlikeliest and best things possible.

☆☆☆

A few days later, Ben arrived at the coffee shop looking much less bruised and battered than he had at the hospital, but still sporting a cast on his arm that stretched from his hand to above his elbow, and with a wan color to his features that made him look much more fragile than he ever had before the accident.

Once they'd exchanged hellos, Martin finally had the chance to make the offer that had been on his mind for weeks. "I asked you in here because I want to know if you'd like a job. A paying one."

Ben's only reply was to gape at Martin.

"It's nothing big, just a few shifts a week. I don't want to overload you while you're getting the hang of things with your arm," Martin explained. "But I thought it might be something that you'd be interested in."

"I...this doesn't make any sense. Why would you offer me a job? You barely know me."

Martin shrugged. "So I'll get to know you."

He'd done rudimentary sums of profit and loss—scribbled on the back of an envelope—to make sure that the new hires wouldn't impact The Warm Taste's ability to cover costs and wages. But the business didn't need to make any more than that. It didn't need to turn a profit for its owner, because Martin had money in his bank account for anything he might need that wasn't covered by the modest wage he paid himself.

His accountant would hate him, but that wasn't anything new. Maybe Martin should pass along the number of Robin's financial manager. The two of them could go out for drinks and despair together over their useless clients.

Ben was still staring at Martin like Martin was an alien.

"Look," Martin told him. "I already know you've got experience working at a place like this. You said so yourself."

"Yeah, I told you that so I could volunteer, not so you'd employ me!"

"You are the first kid I've ever heard of who's worked so hard to flunk a job interview."

Martin's joking words made Ben look abashed. "I don't want you to think I don't appreciate it. I do. I one hundred percent do. I just feel like it's not fair that I'm getting this chance as a result of fucking my life up so badly. It doesn't seem fair to all the people who don't fuck up, you know?"

Martin shrugged. "Life's not fair. We don't get rewarded or punished like we feel we might deserve. You just gotta go on anyway."

Ben gave Martin an impulsive hug, awkward because of the cast but clearly sincere.

"I want you to know that you're a saint," Ben said. "A literal saint."

Martin laughed. "I've heard it on pretty solid authority that the saints don't want the first thing to do with people like me, but thanks for the kind thought."

Martin hoped that when Ben next felt things weighing him down, having people around him would be at least a little bit of a help. Knowing there were people he could reach out to if he wanted to talk could, maybe, be enough for Ben, even if he never went so far as to actually speak to any of them about any of it.

Robin and Martin went out to dinner again, with Robin choosing another simple dish.

"I mean, you're used to eating, so it probably doesn't occur to you that it's incredibly weird, mashing up food with your teeth and then swallowing it. It's a weird, weird thing."

"It's adorable to see you relearn human things."

"I am not adorable," Robin huffed adorably.

"If you say so." Martin laughed and took another mouthful of his meal. Robin did the same, making faces as he chewed, finally swallowing with a look of accomplishment.

"You know that blog post I wrote, the one about night school?"

"Yeah?"

"I'm thinking of maybe trying it, after all. Around writing; how to do nonfiction creatively and things like that. I'm not going to assume that it's too exhausting for me until I give it a try first. As my mother used to say, there's no sense in borrowing trouble."

"That's...that's really good to hear, Robin." Martin could feel his mouth widen into a huge smile.

"Which part?"

"Huh?" Martin gave Robin a puzzled look.

"Oh, come on," Robin teased. "You know what I mean. Are you glad to hear about the night school or glad to hear me mention my family in a way that's not depressing and wistful?"

"Okay, you caught me. But can't I be happy about both? Because I am. I'm happy about both."

Robin gave Martin a grin of his own. "I'm not going to

compare myself to anyone else anymore. My brother's writing was his, and mine is mine. They don't have to be competing with one another. Just because other people used to hold me up to his legacy after they found out who I was doesn't mean I have to do the same thing to myself."

Robin looked down at his plate, giving a quiet laugh. "If writing the blog, and all the metaphors people keep being sure are there on purpose has taught me anything, it's that everyone sees what they need to see. Those readers all those years ago needed to see my brother's talent live on somehow, and they sought it in my own writing. That's all. It's not my responsibility to live up to that."

Chapter Nine

Robin

Robin arrived at The Warm Taste in the early evening, while he was still feeling a little muzzy from sleep. He could see that Sarah was teaching Ben where the different ingredients were stored in the counter area—syrups, toppings, different types of milk—and so he waited until they were done with the lesson before going over, raising a hand in a small wave to Ben as he did so.

"How're you going?" Robin asked by way of greeting. "Sorry, I bet you've been asked that a thousand times by everyone else already."

"Yeah, pretty much," conceded Ben. "But it's okay. I know it's because people care. Or I try to remind myself that they care—it's not something I'm quite ready to call 'knowing' yet. That makes no sense, does it?"

"It makes perfect sense. Don't worry about it," Robin assured him. "I know exactly what you mean; how fucked up and impossible it feels when it suddenly starts to dawn on you that people give a shit about you."

"Yeah, that's it. All these people who give a shit, and I had no idea that they even knew who I was or thought about me from one week to the next. It's kind of a head trip." Ben scratched at his chin with his undamaged hand. "It feels like a big responsibility, too. Like I have to take better care of myself from now on, because there's all these people who want to know if I'm okay. And because

141

I never want to go to a hospital again, if I can help it. Hospitals suck."

"I hear you on that one," agreed Robin emphatically. "I guarantee you I could beat literally any horror story you had about hospitals; don't even ask."

Ben laughed. "Yeah, I don't even want to know, so I'll just trust you on that one."

Surprising himself, Robin felt genuinely touched by the throwaway reply. Trust wasn't something he'd deserved from anyone for a long, long time...but, maybe, he was beginning to become someone worthy of it again. Little by little, he was gaining integrity.

"Can I get you something? I can't promise it'll be perfect, since I'm still learning, but if it sucks you can have it on the house," Ben offered.

Floundering, Robin just picked a random option off the menu board, waiting as Ben prepared his choice. He wondered, for the first time, if it was going to taste any good.

He found himself a seat when his drink was ready. The position of the table was further away from the door than Robin tended to take, if he could help it. His instinct was to be as close to a quick getaway as possible.

But The Warm Taste was safe; he didn't need to be on constant alert for a swift exit. Robin wanted his instincts to start shifting away from the dull, simple choices they'd restricted him to for so long.

He was going to teach himself a better way of existing.

☆☆☆

Robin was a half chapter into the book he'd decided to try reading—a collection of George Orwell's essays—when Martin showed up at the coffee shop. Instead of going straight to work behind the counter, he joined Robin at the table for a few minutes first.

"I'm going to have to try ordering a lot of different choices from your menu on different visits," Robin said. "Otherwise I'm never going to be able to tell which one is actually my favorite. Though, if they're all as nice as this one, choosing is going to be difficult."

"You sound surprised that it's nice," noted Martin. "Did you expect that my coffee shop wouldn't have good coffee?"

Robin ignored the question. "I like this place," he said instead. "I think I might start coming here to study when I'm going to night school. I hope the owner's not too insufferable."

Martin grinned. "I heard he's a dirty old man. He'll probably try to sleep with you."

"Gross." Robin made a theatrically over-the-top face of disgust. Then, dropping the joke, his tone turned serious. "Do you remember when I told you that you bring out the least Gothic and torrid parts of me?"

"Yeah."

"Well, the other half of that truth is that you bring out the most human parts of me. The very parts that I never wanted brought out, frankly. And you...you made me glad of them."

Martin gave Robin a crooked grin. "I'll remember you said that, when the semester's in full swing, and you're violently cursing my name."

"But even that will be good. Even the bad things will be good. Because frustration and struggle are living, vital feelings. They'll remind me that I'm involved with the world, not just hanging back to watch."

"I'll remember you said that, too."

Robin pouted. "I'm trying to be sincere and heartfelt here, and you're just humoring me."

Martin stood. "Yep." He planted a kiss on Robin's forehead and went off toward the counter.

Robin watched after him as he went. It seemed so long ago that Robin's world had revolved around observing Martin, following him as close and silent as a shadow as he went about the details of his life.

In reality it had been several months, which should have felt like nothing after such a long span of existence. But the changes those months had brought, to Robin's routines and to Robin himself, were profound.

The fundamental shift, from feeling as if he was merely existing to something that at least approximated living, was all down to one key new factor: love. Not only in the romantic sense— any relationship based on a desire for the happiness and well-being of another, the wish to help them accomplish that happiness, was love in Robin's opinion though he was fairly sure that wasn't exactly what humans meant by the term.

Maybe that was as close as a vampire could come to truly understanding the feeling, but it felt like a good start to Robin.

None of that meant love was more intrinsically pleasant than the numbness he'd existed in before. Far from it, because the number of terrible risks and opportunities for heartbreak that love brought with it was huge.

And all that was even before the simple ability love had for derailing the expected route of someone's life. All of Robin's old plans and routines, such as they were, had been rendered completely irrelevant.

But one thing Robin was becoming increasingly certain of was that, while love wasn't automatically more pleasant than just existing, it was more worthwhile.

Robin thought that Martin had probably always known and believed that. Even in the worst and most alone moments of his life, when hope seemed like the smallest speck of light in a universe too vast and cold to notice it, Martin had still believed love was worth its price.

Robin wasn't quite there, yet. He wasn't as naturally optimistic as Martin was. Neither of them believed that going through pain and suffering somehow earned anyone a greater right to joy further down the line, but Martin had a gratitude toward his suffering regardless, one that Robin hadn't quite managed to find within himself.

"It brought me to this moment, to the life I have now," Martin had explained to him, as they lay together in the soft gray light of encroaching morning one day. "All the sorrows I had along the way were just that: the way. If I hadn't walked that path, I'd be in a different place now. So I have to be grateful for the sad things, because I'm grateful for where I am, and those are the things that led me here."

Robin could understand that perspective, even if he didn't entirely share it. He was too skilled in compartmentalizing his experiences to perceive, let alone appreciate, a direct line of cause and effect between the various things that had happened to him over the years. His personal time line was too segmented.

That was one of Robin's strongest survival mechanisms, he was sure—the inability to truly conceive of how long his lifespan was—but it was a shame that it cut him off from being able to see the world as Martin did.

He knew that this brief bright flare of happiness would be over soon enough, and then the lonely dark that came after would be all the harder to bear for the light that had come before. And yet, somehow, the knowledge didn't weigh on Robin's heart the way it would have done under the old status quo. He wasn't afraid of what was to come.

The door opened and Polly appeared, waving hello to her

mother and Ben behind the counter and then glancing around to see which of her numerous claimed tables was available. She caught sight of Robin and came over, joining him at his table. Clearly his willingness to sit through several key entries from the Ghibli back catalogue of films had endeared him to her.

"Can I try a sip of your coffee?" she asked without bothering to say hello.

Robin nodded, sliding it toward her across the table.

"Sure, but just a sip. You shouldn't have too much caffeine."

Polly made an annoyed face at his words. "If having caffeine at night is so bad, how come there are so many adults drinking coffee in here right now?"

"I would have thought a kid would know better than anyone that adults are idiots," Robin replied blithely. Polly grinned and then took a small taste of his drink.

"Ugh, that's gross. You should put sugar in it," she decided. "Hey, Robin?"

"Hmm?"

"You're in love with Martin, right?"

Robin nodded. "Yes."

"Cool. He's nice." Polly looked pleased. "If you make him sad, I'm pretty sure my mom's gonna ruin your life. She can do that, you know."

"I absolutely believe that," Robin assured her.

"She caught me when I'd downloaded an R-rated movie once, and she took away my Internet for a week. A week." Polly shuddered at the memory. "And the movie wasn't even all that good. It was weird and sad, mostly. If something's going to have an R rating it should be worth it. A week without anything online was torture."

"Sarah's just trying to protect you from stuff you're not ready for."

Polly made a nearly identical face to her earlier coffee-is-gross expression. "Like how she doesn't want me to know that Ben wanted to die? I've been in and out of hospitals my whole life! It's not like I don't know about death."

"I don't think that was to protect you from knowing about death. I think that was because she didn't want you to know about that facet of life—she might have thought it was too weird and sad, like the movie she didn't want you watching."

"Whatever. That's stupid. I don't need to be old to understand that stuff: living is cool, and anyone who forgets that living is cool needs to get reminded about it."

That made Robin give Polly a small smile. "You think it's that simple?"

"Yep." Polly nodded. "Martin says most stuff is, if you stop expecting it to be complicated. When people are sick, they need to go to hospitals, and when they're sad they need to be where people care about them. That's why Ben went to the hospital and then came here."

"And what if that's not enough?"

Polly shrugged one shoulder. "You keep trying until it is, I guess. You keep loving and you keep trying. That's all. I bet that's what Martin would say."

Robin glanced around him, at the bustling, welcoming energy of The Warm Taste; a place that had drawn him in and given him somewhere to belong, against every expectation he might have had.

He looked at Martin behind the counter, chatting to Sarah and laughing, full of life and generosity and compassion, who had made Robin feel worthy of being saved from himself, despite everything he'd done.

Keep loving and keep trying. It was that simple, once you stopped expecting it to be complicated.

"Yeah," said Robin. "I think you're right."

About the Author

Julia Leijon fell in love with writing at the age of twelve, and with vampires a year later. Despite being in her midthirties now, very little has changed.

Her one moment of infidelity was when she was eighteen and read *Harry Potter and the Prisoner of Azkaban,* briefly switching her allegiance over to werewolves in the aftermath. Though she still writes shifters and weres from time to time, Julia now counts herself as a permanent member of Team Vampire.

Email: julia@julialeijon.com
Website: http://julialeijon.com
Mailing list: Sign up via http://www.captive-princess.com/julia/

NineStar Press, LLC

www.ninestarpress.com

www.ingramcontent.com/pod-product-compliance
Lightning Source LLC
Chambersburg PA
CBHW020340260626
47156CB00004B/1625